Backwards Moon

Backwards Moon

Mary Losure

Holiday House / New York

HOLIDAY HOUSE is registered in the U.S. Patent and Trademark Office.
Printed and Bound in June 2014 at Maple Press, York, PA, USA.
www.holidayhouse.com
1 3 5 7 9 10 8 6 4 2

Library of Congress Cataloging-in-Publication Data
Losure, Mary.
Backwards moon / by Mary Losure. — First edition.
pages cm
Summary: When the magical veil that protects their valley from humans is broached and the Wellspring Water needed to repair it is polluted, it is up to two young witches, Bracken and Nettle, to save the coven.
ISBN 978-0-8234-3160-1 (hardcover : alk. paper) [1. Witches—Fiction. 2. Magic—Fiction.] I. Title.
PZ7.L9Bac 2014
[Fic]—dc23
2013045643

For DCL,
Witchfriend extraordinaire then, now, and always

Backwards Moon

chapter one

It was a good day for flying: pale blue sky, wispy clouds, gentle updrafts. It was also the last ordinary day before everything changed forever.

Nettle didn't know that, but then, you never do.

Bracken, her cousin, wanted to visit the marmots. "We can just *talk* to them," said Bracken. "What's wrong with sitting and talking?"

"On a day like this?" said Nettle. "On a *perfect* day for the Raven Game?"

"Fine." Bracken sighed as they glided over the Least and Middle Meadows. Soon they were flying toward slopes of bare, tumbled rock.

Like all witches, they had deep violet-blue eyes and black hair. They wore it in two long braids, which was the way you did before you turned fifteen. Nettle was small and quick and stubborn. Bracken, even though she was older and taller, tended not to argue with her.

They flew higher, toward dark fir forests. In the distance

rose the jagged, snowy tips of the mountains that ringed the valley.

"You call the ravens," said Nettle. "You're better at it."

Bracken gave a piercing whistle. A moment later, four ravens lifted out of the forest.

"Nice," said Nettle softly. She and Bracken bowed their tall-pointed hats in greeting, then ravens and witches spiraled upward into the dome of the sky.

Nettle liked the Raven Game. There was a rhythm to it: dive, soar, dive. Nettle's stomach always dropped thrillingly before she shot back upward. Sometimes as they dove they let themselves tumble over and over in the air. The ravens always laughed their throaty raven laughs, their claws extended in a most undignified fashion. They did it over and over again, until everyone but Nettle tired of it. Then the ravens looked at each other, gave a few parting caws, and flapped away.

"Did you ever notice how they never say anything?" said Bracken. "I wish at least *sometimes* we could talk to them."

"You can't talk to ravens," said Nettle. "They won't stay still long enough."

"I wish there were some combination of ravens and marmots."

Nettle raised her eyebrows. "Flying marmots? Tunneling ravens?"

"You know what I mean," said Bracken soberly. "Someone who would talk to us *and* be fun to play with."

"Yes. Well," said Nettle, looking away. They hovered for a minute, their faces still, and Nettle knew they were both thinking the same thing: how all the other witches in the valley were long past any kind of game except the kind you play sitting around a table after supper. They were not just old, they were *very* old. Some were hundreds of years old.

It was late now. Shadows had spread across the rock slopes. Soon the mountains would be silhouetted against the glowing sky, their snowy tips tinged with pink. "Maybe tomorrow we can play Catapult," said Nettle. "Catapult works fine with just two."

Bracken nodded and pulled her black hat low on her forehead. Not to stop it falling off, because it wouldn't, being magic. It was just something she did when she was thinking about The Way Things Were. Nettle pulled hers down too. Then with one motion, they wheeled their broomsticks toward home.

chapter two

Nettle and Bracken followed a stream, silver in the fading light. It flowed through thickets of willow bushes, then dropped to the clear pools where the two of them often swam. Lower still, the stream widened to a river that wound in broad bends across the valley floor. When they came to Five Herons Marsh, they turned due east. Then they slowed their brooms and skimmed above the forest.

It was dark now, but with their Nightseeing, Nettle and Bracken could make out an open spot just ahead. They glided low over pumpkin vines and rows of corn. In the daylight, the cornstalks would be tawny and the pumpkins golden, but now they looked gray, yet clear in every detail, the way things did with Nightseeing.

In another moment Nettle could make out stone roofs, cone-shaped like witches' hats, here and there among the oak branches. Crooked chimneys and many-paned gable windows glinted palely in the starlight.

Nettle and Bracken landed on the small, circular clearing

that was the village Commons and swung off their broomsticks. The scent of wood smoke lingered pleasantly in the air. From a front porch a distant banjo twanged, clear and merry, mixing with the faint murmur of old voices and high, cracked laughter.

Nettle and Bracken ran lightly across the Commons and up their own front steps. No light shone inside, which meant that their Great-Aunt Iris was out on somebody else's porch. Their aunt, who loved them dearly but tended to forget things, would be home when she thought of it.

Nettle and Bracken pushed open the door. A pot of lentil stew, now cold, sat on the back of the stove. Still, Nettle liked lentils, and it wouldn't take long to warm them up. She piled wood and kindling, lit them with a spark from her finger, and shut the stove door with a clang.

Bracken put on the kettle for meadow-mint tea and lit the lantern that hung above the table. It made a warm, golden light—much cheerier than gray Nightseeing.

Nettle ate her supper quickly, thinking about which aspen grove they should go to the next day and how to choose the right sapling, with just the right springiness. She imagined the biggest rock they could fling and the clatter and boom it would make as it bounced crazily down the slopes. . . . Catapult was a fine, fine game.

They washed the dishes—it was too bad that magic wouldn't stoop to bothersome everyday tasks—and set them back in the cupboard. Nettle went out on the porch to toss the dishwater out, *whoosh*, and stood for a moment. Above her untold numbers of stars glittered among the oaks' crooked branches. The Cat's Highway arched through them, a starry path that seemed to come from, and go to, the world on the other side of the mountains. As she often did, Nettle imagined herself flying along it. Then she went inside, her bare feet padding softly on the wooden floor, and climbed the ladder to the sleeping loft she shared with her cousin.

Bracken was already in bed, reading the *Cyclopedia of World History* by the light of a single candle. It was the only human-made book in the entire village. Bracken had read it over and over.

Nettle had read it too, though only once. She'd studied all the pictures.

"Where are you now?" Nettle asked as she hung her hat on the bedpost.

"The part where they invent the steam locomotive and the telegraph," said Bracken. So she was nearly at the end.

Nettle stepped out of her dress and left it lying on the floor.

"You're not going to brush your hair?" said Bracken without looking up.

"No," said Nettle, and slipped into bed. She waited while Bracken read the last few pages of the book, which were all about Onward and Upward and the bright future of Mankind from this glorious day forward.

Bracken closed the book and stared into the distance, picking absently at the blanket on her lap. Nettle could tell from her troubled look that Bracken was thinking about their parents and where they had gone.

Nettle's and Bracken's fathers—like all witches' fathers—were Woodfolk. When a Woodfolk man and a witch got married, their children were always tiny witches, with dark violet-blue eyes and spikey black hair. But long ago, when Nettle and Bracken were only babies, their fathers had vanished, along with the entire Woodfolk tribe. Their mothers had gone looking for them, and then they too had vanished.

And ever since, no one would ever talk about it.

"I don't think humans had anything to do with why our parents are gone," said Nettle now.

Bracken didn't say anything.

"Humans have no magic," said Nettle.

Bracken shrugged.

"Bracken, they can't even *see* us."

"Human *children* can," said Bracken.

"They can't be all that dangerous," said Nettle. "And what about Witchfriends?" (Witchfriends were special humans who, even when they were grown up, could see witches.) "There's no need to be afraid of *them,* obviously."

"Then why do we live so far away from the human world?" asked Bracken, as she had a hundred times before. "If humans are harmless, why would Rose and Scabiosa and the rest go to all the trouble of spell-spinning a Veil across the pass to keep them out?"

"I think it's to keep *us* in," said Nettle. Because it was true: whenever they flew too close to the pass that led to the outside world, their broomsticks turned around of their own accord.

"But *why*?" asked Bracken.

It was no use asking. Rose (who was sort of the leader of the village but not really, since witches didn't believe in having leaders) would only gaze at you with her deep, old eyes and say there was no telling what the humans were up to these days and she for one didn't want to find out. Somebody else would change the subject, and that would be that.

It was obvious that the older witches had decided not to answer certain questions. Perhaps they'd done it late at night, all sitting around the Gathering Fire, in accordance with the ancient tradition of witch decision-making. Though in practice this always led to a lot of time-consuming arguing. . . .

So maybe it was just something Rose or Scabiosa had

decided and the rest went along with, as often happened. But in any case, it came out to the same thing: it was no use asking.

"I think we should ask the wolves," said Bracken. "They've been through the pass lots of times. They must know about humans."

"Yes," said Nettle, sitting up.

And at that very moment, a wolf howled.

Far away in the night, a second wolf answered. A chorus of yips and barks rose, then faded away.

"See?" said Bracken. "It's an omen."

And maybe it was, though not the way they thought.

chapter three

Neither Nettle nor Bracken had ever actually talked to a wolf, and even spotting one was never easy. Bracken thought they would be easiest to find in the meadows, but she and Nettle had flown all day and not seen one. Wolves were clever that way.

Nettle thought they'd be on the bare rock slopes below the peaks, but Bracken said they weren't there, obviously. Did she see any?

"What would be so wrong with just flying up closer?" said Nettle.

"It's late," said Bracken, in that annoying I Am Older voice she sometimes used. "We have to get home."

"We do not," said Nettle. "Aunt Iris won't even remember we're gone. And besides, we wasted all day looking where they weren't. Now let's go where *I* wanted to go."

"Oh, all right," said Bracken. So they flew higher.

"See?" said Bracken finally. "Now let's go home." She turned around and skimmed toward the village.

Nettle took one last look at the slopes. Then she stopped, hovering.

"Bracken, wait!" she called.

Bracken made a graceful swoop around.

"Look *there!*" said Nettle, pointing. Two tiny, distant shapes were making their way, very slowly, down the slope.

"Those aren't wolves," said Bracken, staring. "They're walking on two legs. And they're wearing trousers!"

Nettle caught her breath. "Bracken! Do you think they might be...?" She glanced at her cousin, hardly daring to hope.

Bracken shook her head. "They're not Woodfolk. They can't be! Look at the way they move, so slow and heavy. Nobody magic would move like that."

"Oh," said Nettle dully. She felt sick with disappointment.

"I would know Woodfolk if I saw them," said Bracken quietly. "I would know them *instantly.*"

Nettle squeezed her eyes tightly shut and rubbed them with her sleeve. Then she stared, again, at the slope.

The tiny figures plodded steadily lower, picking their way around boulders and edging across falls of broken, loose stone. A rock dislodged by their feet clattered down the mountainside, the sound echoing across the vast landscape.

"Nettle, those are *humans*!" said Bracken. "They can only be humans."

Nettle turned to stare at her. "But...how could one get in?"

"Something must have gone wrong with the Veil."

"But how...?"

"I don't *know,*" said Bracken fiercely. They hovered, staring. "Maybe we should go back and tell the others."

"I want to see one," said Nettle. "They can't see us. What's the harm? Come on," she said, and flew toward them.

"*Nettle,*" said Bracken, but she followed.

A shrill cry sounded above them. *Kree! Kree! Kree!* A hawk circled high in the sky, peering down at the humans.

They were men, both of them. They had big, heavy-looking bundles on their backs and wore odd little caps with brims like ducks' bills. And their feet were not bare, like witches' feet. Their toes were trapped in . . . in . . . what? *Boots*, Nettle thought they were called.

Nettle leaned down. "Humans?" she called.

The walkers stopped. Their eyes—which were a strange pale blue, not the deep violet-blue of witches' eyes—looked toward the sound, unseeing.

"Did you hear that?" cried one. His hair was the color of sand.

The two humans peered upward nearsightedly, like moles.

"Yes," said the other, bigger one.

"Did it sound like . . . a voice?' " asked the sandy-haired one. "Sort of a high voice. A girl's voice."

"They *can't* see us!" whispered Nettle. "They really can't!" It was amazing, being invisible. She liked it.

"Listen!" said Sandyhair, stopping. "It's like . . . like ghosts," he muttered.

"That's ridiculous," said Big One, but now they walked faster, glancing all around.

"Humans?" said Nettle again, but this time she had switched to the Language: the silent way of talking, like thoughts traveling, that you used when you talked with animals. "Oh, humans?" she called again in the Language, but they only hurried forward.

"Hello?" said Nettle in the Language.

Her skin prickled. It was odd, not being seen *or* heard.

"Check the GPS again," said the first human suddenly.

Big One pulled out a little flat box.

"What's that thing he's holding?" said Nettle in the Language. She hovered nearer, trying to see.

"It must be one of their inventions!" replied Bracken in the Language.

With his thumb, Big One jabbed at the box. "This makes no sense," he said. "It's like this valley isn't even on the map. There's still only this blank, blurry space."

"Really?" said Sandyhair. "Could it be out of satellite range?"

"I don't see how." Big One jabbed the box again, then stuck it in his pocket before Nettle had time to see.

"Drat," she muttered.

"There's something creepy about this valley," said Sandyhair. "I think we should turn back."

"But... it's so *beautiful,*" said Big One softly. He gazed out over the vast sweep of forest and meadow, to distant waterfalls that hung like white threads against the cliffs.

"I've hiked all over the world," he said slowly. "And I've never seen wilderness like this. Never."

The hawk's high, shrill call sounded again. It swooped lower, hovered near Nettle and Bracken, and glared at them with its fierce yellow-ringed eyes. "What's wrong with you two? What are you waiting for? Get rid of them!"

"Get *rid* of them?" said Nettle, gaping.

The hawk nodded grimly.

chapter four

"You mean *kill* them?" gasped Nettle.

"Witches don't just... kill things," said Bracken slowly.

"*Stun* them, then," snapped the hawk. "Get them out of here." He jerked his sharp, curved beak at the humans. "Use those finger sparks of yours." He soared higher and circled around, his wings beating the air.

Nettle and Bracken stared at each other.

"I stunned a rabbit I was mad at, once," said Nettle slowly.

"You did?" said Bracken, startled.

"He was *fine*. Well, later he was."

Bracken furrowed her forehead.

"*I'll* do it," said Nettle. She swooped down, aimed her index finger at Sandyhair, and shot out a long silver spark. He fell to a sitting position, toppled sidewise, and slid to a stop on the sloping ground.

Big One stared down at him, goggle-eyed.

Nettle shot another spark. Big One sank, slid, and came to

rest with his bundle underneath him. He looked like a turtle turned upside down.

"Are they breathing?" gasped Bracken, landing.

"They're . . . fine," said Nettle nervously. And they really did seem to be.

The hawk dived down, his sharp talons reaching toward the limp and helpless humans. Then he veered away. Next to the humans' bulk, he looked like a delicate bundle of feathers and bones, Nettle noticed with a shock. His eyes were like dark glass.

"Truss them up!" he shrieked. "Get them out of here!"

"It's all right," said Nettle gently.

"Go back to the village!" Bracken told him. "Go tell the others."

The hawk gave them a glassy stare, then lifted off with a shrill cry.

"We need a way to carry them." Nettle rummaged for her hammock.

"Here." Bracken pulled hers from her well-ordered pocket. Like all witches' pockets, it hung smooth, without a bulge, and weighed nothing no matter what you put in it.

"Humans look bigger up close than they do from the air," said Nettle. They also looked heavier.

"Maybe you should have thought of that before you stunned them," said Bracken.

"Me!" said Nettle. "The hawk said to stun them, so I did. Give me the hammock." Nettle spread it next to the smaller human, Sandyhair. "Careful, now." They rolled him onto the netting.

"Now the other," said Nettle. But Big One, in his upside-down-turtle position, was harder. After much grunting, futile heaving, and arguing, Nettle thought of using their broomsticks as levers, which did the trick.

"We should tie them in. We don't want them to fall," said Bracken. She reached in her pocket.

"Look here." Nettle pulled at an end trailing from Big One's bundle.

It turned out to be a whole coil of rope. It was not rough brown like all the rope they'd ever seen, but white—thin and smooth and light.

"I wonder what this is made of," said Bracken, fingering it.

"I bet they have other things in their bundles," said Nettle.

"We don't have time to rummage through their bundles," said Bracken. "Besides, it doesn't seem right."

They roped the humans securely into the hammock, then each cousin fastened one end of it to her broomstick with a swift, well-tied knot.

"They're so *helpless,*" said Nettle. "How can everyone be afraid of them? That's what I don't understand."

"It does seem odd," admitted Bracken.

The humans swung gently as Nettle and Bracken soared, rather heavily, toward the pass. It was a deep cleft between two familiar peaks, Gaia's Summit and Badger's Nose.

"Does the pass look different to you?" asked Nettle.

Bracken nodded slowly. "It's because the Veil is broken."

It was as though some sadness hung in the air, like something you couldn't quite remember. A scent, or a tune, or a way you'd once felt.

They flew higher. Night began to fall and the air grew colder. Wisps of mist drifted past. Now, below them, patches of snow lay in the shelter of giant boulders. Nettle leaned down.

"Look! Their tracks," she said to Bracken, pointing to a smudgy line in the snow. "Their boot tracks."

They glided toward the cleft. Walls of rock loomed on

either side. A damp, cold smell filled their noses. And then, just like that, they were on the other side! The gray rock slopes now led down instead of up.

In the distance lay another valley. It was deeply wooded, just like the one they'd come from. Like their own valley, this one was ringed by mountains, though these had unfamiliar outlines and no names that they knew.

Above them the first stars pricked out. They flew through the growing dark, looking for a place to set the humans down.

"Is this far enough, do you think?" asked Nettle.

"I guess so," said Bracken.

They landed and lowered the hammock to the stony ground.

"I think we should do a forgetting spell on them, so they don't tell other humans," said Bracken.

"You do it," said Nettle. Bracken was good at spells. Better than Nettle would ever be.

Bracken put her fingers to her cheeks and closed her eyes. " 'Misting spell, misting spell,' " she muttered to herself, and Nettle knew she was trying to remember the words of one of the harder forgetting spells, a tricky one that Nettle had read but not bothered to learn.

One of the humans stirred and groaned.

"They're waking up!" said Nettle. The humans opened their eyes. "Cast the spell!" she cried, forgetting to use the Language. The humans stiffened with terror.

Quickly, Bracken spread her fingers and held them over the humans. " 'Calmly, calmly, walk the way,' " she chanted in a high, nervous voice. " 'Take your path, and choose it wisely. Know ye that your way's your own, of your own choosing, clear and bright.' "

The humans lay very still. Their wide, startled pupils reminded Nettle of a rabbit who's hoping you don't see him.

"'Long the path, and winds betimes...'" continued Bracken, but as she finished the spell, her voice, too, was calm, and Nettle could tell she was ready for the next step.

Bracken twirled three times, her braids flying, then stood with her arms outstretched, gazing upward. She breathed—in and out, in and out—then from her breathing came the rest of the forgetting spell. Some parts were out loud, some in the Language.

She seemed, as far as Nettle could tell, to be getting every word right, even the ending.

The spell hung in the air like mist.

"Human beings," said Bracken steadily. "You will forget, soon, everything about the pass you crossed and the valley you saw."

The humans nodded dumbly.

"You will go home now. You will retrace your steps to wherever it is that you came from."

The humans' heads bobbed in time to Bracken's voice.

"If you ever wonder why something happened on your journey, you will believe it was for some ordinary reason." Bracken leaned down close. "You will never go back to our valley. You will never tell any other human it exists. Go now." She bowed, her hat-point making a small arc against the black, star-scattered sky. "Fare-thee-well and merry be."

The humans blinked, then tried to sit up.

"The knots!" said Bracken in the Language.

Nettle darted forward. The humans lay calmly as she undid every knot. Then they sat up.

"We need our headlamps," said Big One to Sandyhair.

Moving slowly and fumblingly—humans didn't seem to see at all well in the dark—each retrieved something from his bundle and fastened it to his forehead.

"My!" gasped Bracken, squinting, as from each forehead shot a bright beam of light.

The men turned their heads this way and that, the light beams playing over the boulders.

"All right, now. I remember exactly how we came," said Big One.

"So do I," said Sandyhair. "We can make camp in a couple of hours. Get an early start tomorrow. Be back to the truck by nightfall. Home on Wednesday, most likely."

"Sure," said Big One. "It will be good to be home."

The two men hefted their bundles and walked off into the night.

"I wish we could have talked to them," said Nettle. "Don't you?"

"No," said Bracken slowly.

"Aren't you even curious?"

"It gives me a funny feeling, seeing humans," said Bracken.

Nettle bent down to pick up Bracken's hammock and paused. Something small and dark and square lay nearby on the stony ground. "Hey," she said. "Look! It's that Invention. The black box!" She snatched it up and jabbed at it, the way the human had done.

Then they both froze, transfixed.

The box emitted a very faint, high whine. Then, on its glassy surface, a strange hard light shone.

"Drop it!" cried Bracken.

The box landed with its square of light facedown, but a glow leaked out from the edges.

"It's like . . . magic!" said Bracken in a hollow voice.

"It can't be," said Nettle. "Humans don't have magic. They can't! They don't."

They stared until the glow and the whine faded away.

Nettle nudged the box with her toe. Nothing happened. "I think we should take it with us. I think we should show the others."

"Pick it up, then. *Don't* jab it," Bracken added quickly.

"I'm *not,*" said Nettle. She slipped it into her pocket.

"It made the same kind of light as those things they wore on their heads," said Bracken uneasily. "Hard. Cold."

They watched as the mysterious headlights bobbed slowly down the slope. "Nettle?" said Bracken suddenly. "Look down there." Way past the humans, far down the valley, shone more lights, tiny in the distance.

They were not the soft yellow glow of candles, or firelight, or lamplight. They were white and cold and hard.

"They're not moving," said Bracken. She paused. "Could those be lights from human *cottages*? A whole *village* of humans?"

"I think they must be!"

"A human village," said Bracken slowly.

"Bracken, let's go see!"

Bracken frowned.

"Now!" said Nettle. "Bracken, if we don't go now, we might never get to! Rose will fix the Veil, and we'll be trapped again. Forever!" She pulled out her broomstick. "Come *on*!"

"We don't have much time," said Bracken worriedly as they sped along. "The hawk will have told the others by now. They'll be coming, and if they find out we've gone all the way down here we're going to be in really, really big trouble."

"They won't find out," said Nettle. "And I want to see something different! I want to see something *new*, and you do too."

"Fine," muttered Bracken.

But as they flew toward the human village, Nettle could see that there were many more lights than she'd expected. Some of them blinked, and some were different colors: red and green and blue.

Bracken slowed her broomstick. "Everything is strange here. Nettle, come on. I think we should go."

Nettle hovered, staring.

"Nettle, if you don't come, I'm going home without you. I mean it," said Bracken.

Nettle wheeled her broomstick around.

chapter five

They had just cleared the pass and had turned toward the village when Rose came hurtling toward them, her bony shoulders stiff, her long dress fluttering. "What news?" she cried shrilly.

"We sent them home!" said Bracken. "I cast a forgetting spell on them first."

"Did it work?" said Rose sharply.

"Yes," said Bracken.

"Are you *sure*? Are you absolutely sure?"

Bracken hesitated. "I think so. It seemed that way! But Rose, there are lights beyond the pass! Human lights!"

Rose took in a breath through closed teeth. "Come with me," she commanded and swept back through the pass.

She scanned the valley. "*Blast.* Blast and *stink* it."

"It's a village, isn't it?" said Bracken.

Rose nodded grimly. "Go home now, both of you. Right this minute."

"Aren't you coming?" asked Bracken.

"I have an errand to do," said Rose. "Go back. I'll be there soon."

"What if we just wait here?" said Nettle.

"Go home!" said Rose in a terrible voice.

So they did.

On the Commons, the Gathering Fire glowed. Seven black hats and seven sets of bony knees were ringed around it on log benches. Even Great-Aunt Iris was there, huddled with the rest.

Nettle and Bracken glided swiftly toward them. The circle of faces looked up.

"Are they gone?" called Violet. Her voice sounded even higher and tenser than usual.

"Yes," said Bracken, alighting. The others moved aside to make room on the benches. "We cast a forgetting spell on them and sent them back to wherever they came from."

"There were only two?" said Scabiosa. She was a big-shouldered witch with a wide grin and wild hair that was always escaping from its braid. Normally her voice was loud and full of laughter, but now it wasn't. "The hawk said there were only two."

"Yes," said Bracken. "But we saw lights. Human lights, down the valley."

A murmur ran round the circle. "Many?" asked Scabiosa.

"It seemed like a lot," said Bracken.

"Rose met us on the way back, but she didn't come with us," said Nettle. "She said she had an errand to do. She didn't say what kind of errand."

The firelight flickered on haggard faces.

"She's gone to get Wellspring water," Scabiosa said slowly. "Water to fix the Veil."

"See," said Nettle under her breath. "What did I tell you about the Veil?"

"Why . . . why is everyone so *worried?*" asked Bracken.

The wind stirred. The flames of the Gathering Fire wavered.

"You might as well tell them," said a hollow voice. Nettle turned her head, startled. Then, from the darkness outside the circle, Toadflax's bent form stepped into the firelight. She stared at Bracken with hard eyes. "We're doomed," she snapped. "All of us."

"Stop it, Toadflax," said several voices at once. Shrill murmuring and muttering rose.

"What are you *talking* about?" asked Nettle. "That's ridiculous. We'll fix the Veil and everything will be fine!"

Toadflax gave her a tight smile. *"Everything will be fine,"* she mimicked. "Oh yes, we'll be just fine, just like the passenger pigeons were fine. Once they flew in flocks so immense they blackened the sky. But come to think of it, I haven't seen any around lately. Have you?"

"Don't listen to her," said Scabiosa.

"This valley is beautiful *now,*" said Toadflax. She blinked her red-rimmed eyes. "Just like the world outside it was—before the humans ruined it. Like the forests—before they chopped them all down, like the prairies, with wildflowers as far as the eye could see, and lovely long grass blowing in the wind. Now it's all gone, the birds say. Plowed under by humans. We should have fought them when we had the chance, but did we? No! We hid here. *And what will keep them out now, pray tell?"*

"The *Veil,*" said Nettle. "We'll fix the Veil."

"You think so?" Toadflax laughed softly. "How nice for you."

"And besides," said Nettle, "I still don't see why you're all so afraid of humans! I really, really don't."

"Perhaps someone should tell you," said Toadflax.

"No!" said Scabiosa, rising from her seat. "Toadflax, hold your tongue. We have all agreed. We'll tell them when the time is right."

Toadflax snorted. "We have humans coming through the pass, and now isn't the time to tell them? What exactly will it *take,* pray?"

"Silence," said Scabiosa in a voice Nettle had never heard before.

Toadflax stared around the circle, then shrugged. "So be it. Persist in your folly." She spat on the ground and stalked into the night.

"What was she *talking* about?" asked Bracken.

"Never mind," said Violet primly. "Off to bed, you two. We'll wait up for Rose."

"What?" cried Nettle. "This isn't fair." She gazed pleadingly around the circle.

Sedge, the youngest of the old witches, gave her a sympathetic shrug back. Sometimes it seemed as though Sedge and her friend Reed, the second-youngest-of-the-old witches, were the only ones who even vaguely remembered what it was like to be a witchling.

"It's not, you know," Reed said now in her clear voice. "It's *not* fair. I think Nettle and Bracken should be told what's going on."

"You," said Violet, "are a mere one hundred and fifty years old. I don't think it's for you to contradict your elders."

"Oh for pity's sake, Violet," sighed Sedge. She leaned over toward Nettle and Bracken. "We've argued with them," she whispered. "But . . . you . . . know . . . how . . . they . . . are."

"There's no reason anybody has to go to bed if she doesn't want to," said Reed. "It's not far to the Wellspring. If all goes well Rose should be back soon."

"*If* all goes well," said Violet.

"What do you mean, 'if all goes well'?" Nettle asked.

"Enough questions," said Violet, not looking at her.

"But..."

Bracken elbowed Nettle. *"Quiet,"* she muttered. "Goose. You'll get us sent to bed."

"Goose, yourself," whispered Nettle, staring at the fire.

Silence fell.

A log broke and fell into ashes, and still no one said anything.

Nettle's head nodded. She leaned against Bracken and closed her eyes.

Nettle woke to a hubbub of shrill, excited voices. It was first light; everyone was standing up, staring toward a black speck fluttering against the pale sky. As it drew closer, Nettle could make out Rose's hat and broomstick.

"Thank Gaia!" said Scabiosa. "Oh, thank Gaia..."

Rose landed by the now-dead fire and climbed shakily off her broomstick. "I got it," she said, pulling a bottle of water from her pocket. "But they've found the Wellspring. There were houses around it. Lights."

"You weren't seen?" asked Scabiosa quickly.

"No," said Rose. She sank to a seat, her face gray and drawn.

"Is the Wellspring water still good?" asked Violet.

"It was hard to tell in the glare," said Rose, sighing.

"The Veilspinning, it's a nightspell, isn't it?" asked Scabiosa. "We'll have to wait until night to try."

Rose nodded. "Midnight. Oh, my head hurts. I can't think straight..."

"It will be all right, Rose," said Scabiosa, patting her shoulder with one big hand. "You shouldn't worry so. The Veilspinning will work, surely. It's time now to get some sleep."

Everyone stood and bowed their heads, their pointed hats bobbing. "Merry meet, and merry part," they murmured. It was what you always said at the close of a Gathering, merry or not. Then they all turned soberly toward their cottages.

On the edge of the Commons a branch snapped—a tiny sound, but Nettle turned her head. Something small and thin and low to the ground—a weasel? a marten?—seemed to slip into the underbrush and scurry away.

chapter six

Nettle woke to the pleasant smells of meadow-mint tea and wood smoke. Outside the sleeping loft window, the sun was high over Gaia's Summit. For a moment Nettle couldn't think why she would still be abed at this hour. Then she remembered everything.

She looked over at Bracken's bed. It was empty. Nettle stood and slipped on her dress. She snatched her hat from the bedpost and crammed it on her head. Then she climbed swiftly down the ladder. Through the front window, she could see Bracken outside, huddled on the porch swing. Great-Aunt Iris lay fast asleep in her bed by the stove, her thin gray braid trailing on the floor. Nettle snuck past her, slipped through the door, and sat down beside Bracken on the swing. "It's like the whole world has changed. In one day. Because of two humans."

Bracken nodded. "What *is* it about them, that thing that makes them so dangerous that nobody will tell us?"

"Sedge said we should be told. We could ask her."

"She can't," said Bracken. "They've all agreed."

Part of being in a coven meant that when you agreed to something, you stuck to it. But Nettle and Bracken had both noticed that when it came to agreeing on things, some people's opinions seemed to count more than others', and that witchlings didn't get a say at all.

"Bother," muttered Nettle.

"Toadflax wanted to tell us," said Bracken.

"We could try asking her," said Nettle.

"But how could we find her? It's no use going to her cottage."

"True," said Nettle soberly.

Toadflax's cottage was built on a ledge halfway up the cliffs, and whenever you flew near it, the cottage disappeared. Whether you could even see it from the valley floor depended on the time of day: where the sun was, and the light and shadows on the cliff face.

Once, long ago, Nettle had flown up and stared for a long time at the spot where the cottage was supposed to be. But there was something about the shadows, the chill air... Nettle hadn't wanted to land. She thought of that now, as the swing hung still. She didn't feel like swinging.

In the silence, a hermit thrush sang. The notes cascaded down in perfect harmony, a waterfall of sound. Great Aunt Iris's snoring stopped. A gentle bumping, then their aunt padded onto the porch and peered out over the railing. Sunlight filtered through tree leaves and made patches of gold on the forest floor.

"My, what a pretty day," she said. "Are you off to the meadow again? Take some muffins. I made them yesterday, those ones with currants. The kind you both like." Then she turned and frowned, as though she were trying to remember something. "That business with the humans. Did we get it cleared up?"

"Not exactly. Not yet," said Bracken.

Great-Aunt Iris sat down in her rocking chair. "The Veil," she said, rocking back and forth. "It seemed to me they said there was something wrong with it. That can't be right, though. Can it?"

"They're fixing it tonight," said Bracken. "At midnight."

"Good," said Great-Aunt Iris. She leaned back and pushed with her strong, bare toes. The familiar *clunk, clunk, clunk* of her rocker mixed with the usual birdsong, as though this were any ordinary day.

Nettle wanted to go through the pass again, that morning.

"Please," she begged. "It will only be open for today. Just until they fix the Veil. Come on, Bracken. Please."

"I thought you wanted to play Catapult," said Bracken.

"I did, but that was before."

But for once Bracken wouldn't budge. "I think we should stay in the valley. And don't sulk, or I won't play at all."

So Catapult it was.

Nettle fetched some muffins and nuts and cheese and two bottles of blackberry juice and slipped them into her pocket. She had always taken her pocket for granted, but that morning it struck her how awful it would be if it didn't work—if you had to put everything you wanted to carry into a bundle and lug it around on your back. If your only pocket was a pathetic little thing like the ones humans had...

It was then that she remembered the black box.

"The box!" she said. "We forgot about the box!" She pulled it from her pocket and jabbed it. It made its tiny unpleasant whine, but in the daylight its strange glow did not look so sinister.

"Remember how they said it was a map?" said Bracken suddenly. "The two humans, remember? They said it was a map."

"We could use it to explore!" said Nettle.

"Maybe," said Bracken, looking at it doubtfully.

"Let's take it out to the sitting rock," said Nettle. "Come on." She hurried down the porch steps.

The sitting rock was a little way into the forest in a sunny clearing where leathery ferns grew. Nettle sat down and jabbed the box again. It seemed to be growing a bit weary. . . . It took longer for the whine to start and the light to appear. Nettle jabbed it again.

"Don't just keep jabbing," said Bracken. "Think first. There must be some sort of trick to it. . . . Here, let me have it."

Nettle handed it to her.

They jabbed and stared, jabbed and stared. The light went on and off.

"This is making me dizzy," said Nettle. She sighed and looked up from the box. Then she jumped, startled.

A creature peered out of the ferns, its pointed nose quivering. The air wavered, and Toadflax stood before them. "It's no use looking at their maps," she said. "Your way is a witch's way." Toadflax muttered something under her breath. The box sailed through the air and landed at her feet. Before Nettle or Bracken could move, it began to quiver. A series of small fires erupted from its glassy surface. A cloud of foul, acrid smoke drifted and twisted in the sunlit clearing.

Toadflax grinned sourly. "That takes care of *that.*"

"You might have asked!" said Nettle hotly.

Toadflax shrugged.

"What do you mean our way 'is a witch's way'?" said Bracken.

"You'll find out soon enough," said Toadflax. "At the Veilspinning."

"What are you talking about?" snapped Bracken.

" 'Rose, you shouldn't *worry* so,' " Toadflax mimicked in Scabiosa's deep voice. " 'The Veilspinning will work, *surely.*' "

"How did you know she said that?" demanded Nettle. "You were listening in after you left!"

"Of course," said Toadflax.

"You were that marten I saw."

"True," said Toadflax. "And don't you wish you could do a spell like that?"

And with that, the air wavered. A scrabbling, the swish of a long tail, and she was gone.

chapter seven

"She wrecked the box without even asking!" said Nettle. "And I *hate* the way she sneaks around like that, listening and spying."

Bracken nodded. "The others never change form like that. She has way more magic than they do."

"What did she mean, our way is a witch's way?"

Bracken raised her shoulders. "She said we'd find out. Then she made fun of Scabiosa for saying the Veilspinning will work."

"Do you think the others will even let us *come* to the Veilspinning?"

"Probably not," said Bracken.

"They can't keep treating us like little bitty witchlings our whole life. They can't," said Nettle.

But it turned out they could: a Veilspinning was no place for witchlings, Rose said. Which meant they had to stay home.

* * *

It was almost midnight, and out their sleeping loft window, Nettle and Bracken could see dim gray shapes standing in a circle around where the Gathering fire would be if anyone had lit it.

Nettle counted off each pointed hat. "Six," she said. "Seven, eight, nine. That means Toadflax is there. Do you think she's even helping?"

"You would think so," said Bracken. "If only to keep the humans out for her own selfish self."

They watched as each witch took a lantern from her pocket and lit it with a spark from her finger. The lights rose into the sky and hovered. Nettle could hear shrill voices as the group formed a wavering V. Like wild geese on the wing, they streamed toward the pass.

"Now?" asked Nettle, getting out her broomstick. Bracken nodded. They climbed to the window ledge, leaped onto their brooms, and sped after the lanterns.

"Keep back," said Bracken. "Don't get too close."

As they neared the pass, the witches scattered, their lanterns glimmering. Rose gave a sharp cry, and at that, the lanterns soared sidewise across the pass. Behind each lantern a thread of light spooled forth, glowing. Like spiders spinning, the witches glided back and forth and up and down. The strands wove together into a quivering web of light.

"The Veil," breathed Bracken.

The witches were chanting now.

Rose flew above the web, scattering drops from the bottle of Wellspring water. A wind blew down the valley, stirring the threads. Then the chanting died away.

The threads began to dull and fray.

"Something's wrong," muttered Bracken. "Something doesn't seem right. It doesn't feel right."

Scraps of Veil drifted by, gray as cobwebs. Nettle looked to the pass. The sadness she'd noticed before, the hint of a tune not remembered, still seemed to hang there. A wailing, a high-pitched crying under the stars, began. At first Nettle thought it was the wind.

"They're *crying,*" said Bracken in a shocked voice. Nettle and Bracken hovered, horrified, as the others streamed past them, unseeing.

All but one.

"I thought you'd be here," said Toadflax. She hovered near, holding her lantern high.

"It failed!" cried Bracken. "The magic failed."

"I knew it would," said Toadflax. She drew closer. "The Wellspring water was no good," she hissed. "As any fool could have foreseen. The Wellsprings are ruined, ruined by humans with their stink and their noise and their trampling. It's no good hiding here in this poor doomed little valley. Now follow me."

"Follow you?" said Bracken faintly.

Toadflax nodded. "To my cottage. Only to my cottage. I have things to tell you. Things you need to know. Come," she said. "Don't be afraid. I want only the best for you."

Nettle and Bracken stared numbly.

"And the others too!" Toadflax added quickly. "Certainly, certainly the others too! Come, it's not far."

Nettle looked at Bracken.

Bracken pulled her hat down low. "All right," she said.

As they neared the cliff face, Toadflax muttered a spell and landed on the ledge. The outlines of her cottage appeared as if through a drifting fog. There was no front porch, no swing—only a rocky path to a stout wooden door. Toadflax strode forward and waited in the gloom, holding her lantern high.

Nettle and Bracken stowed their broomsticks in their pockets, then followed Toadflax inside.

"Oh!" said Bracken, stopping. Rows and rows of spell books, human-made books, and books that Nettle didn't recognize as either sat on shelves carved deep into the rock.

"Pretty, aren't they?" said Toadflax. "Go ahead. Take a look."

Bracken walked along the shelves, head bent, reading every spine.

"I see you've noticed the *Encyclopedia of Known Enchantments,*" said Toadflax, running a thin finger along the volumes. "It's too bad the others don't have one." She smiled. "It would have been especially useful for Rose. She's the one who gives you your lessons, is she not? But so it goes."

"The *Encyclopedia of Known Enchantments,*" said Bracken slowly. "You had one all this time and you didn't *tell* anybody?"

"Selfish!" said Nettle.

"Don't be impudent," said Toadflax. She hung her lantern on the hook above the table. "Sit down," she said, sinking to a seat. Her face was pale, her eyes shadowed by her hat's wide brim. "The time has come, and then some."

Nettle and Bracken sat on the bench across from her.

"What they won't tell you about is the Fading," said Toadflax.

"The Fading," quavered Bracken. "What's . . . the Fading?"

"The Fading is when you lose your powers," said Toadflax.

"Your *magic* powers?" said Nettle, aghast.

"How could you lose your *powers*?" asked Bracken.

"Humans drain them away," said Toadflax.

"That's impossible. That could never happen!"

"You don't think so?" said Toadflax. "It's happened to many, many covens." She paused. "It began in the days when we lived in the Old Country. In London."

"In London," echoed Bracken bleakly.

"Everyone thought it was a disease, from the stink and roar of the city," said Toadflax. "The oldest ones succumbed first, and then the next oldest, then the next after that. The youngest ones seemed to hold out the longest."

"And . . . they lost their *powers*?" Bracken seemed dazed.

"Yes," hissed Toadflax. She leaned toward them. "*It happens whenever there are too many humans near!* That's why we left the Old Country and came to this one. It's why the Woodfolk came too. They thought they'd be safe." She smiled wanly. "So much for that idea."

"If you lost your powers, you couldn't *fly*!" cried Nettle. She swallowed. "You couldn't talk to animals! You'd have to lug everything around in some big, heavy bundle on your back. . . ."

"Exactly," said Toadflax. "It is too horrible to contemplate. *But that is what will happen to you* when humans come to this valley. As they will, soon." She stared at them with glittering eyes.

Bracken put her head in her hands. "This is awful. Awful."

"Ah, but I have something that might help you," said Toadflax. She got up and went to the cupboard. When she returned she set something down on the table.

It was round—about the size and shape of a loaf of bread—and wrapped in a soft brown cloth embroidered with oak leaves and acorns.

"A seeking stone!" gasped Bracken. "You have a *seeking stone*?"

Seeking stones were old and potent magic. You could gaze

into one and see another witch who had one, even if she was far away.

"I thought the seeking stones were all gone!" said Bracken. "Lost..."

"You were wrong," said Toadflax as she pulled back the cloth.

The stone was a smooth blue-green, veined with darker green. "It takes two stones, working together, to see anything," Toadflax said. "Now, listen closely...."

But Nettle didn't.

She reached out, not thinking, and touched the stone's smooth surface. Instantly, a mist rose and swirled around her.

"Fool!" shrieked Toadflax, but already her voice seemed to come from someplace far away. "Not yet! You little..."

Then came blackness.

chapter eight

Time and space seemed to whoosh together.

The darkness whirled.

When it stopped, Nettle was standing in a vast sunlit room. On the far side, under an archway, stood a gaggle of human children. They were staring at her, eyes goggling, mouths wide open.

"A witch! It's a *witch*!" screamed one. They all began to yell and point.

Nettle stared back, frozen. If one came close she could spark it, but there were so many of them. . . .

"QUIET!" yelled a deep voice. A man and a woman appeared in the archway. "JASON. EMILY! GET BACK HERE! ALL OF YOU! GET BACK HERE RIGHT THIS MINUTE."

"It's a witch!" said a girl, pointing.

"She's standing right there," said a boy.

"Jason, that is not one bit funny," said the man. "Line up, all of you. This field trip is *over*."

"She is, she *is*!" said the girl. "There's a girl right there, and she's wearing a witch costume, and she wasn't there a minute ago."

"Emily, I am surprised at you," said the woman. "Jason, *get back here.*" She grabbed the boy's arm and propelled him back in line.

Nettle held still as a rabbit, watching as the children slouched one behind the other into two long lines.

"Field trips," sighed the man to the woman. "I don't know what gets into them."

The woman glared at the children. "They opened up this whole museum, the entire Atkinson House, on a Friday afternoon *especially for our school*, and this is how you behave?"

Moans, grumbling.

"I don't know who is responsible for this stupid stunt," she said, looking at Jason. "But let me just say it will be a *long time* before you are taken to another museum. AND I WILL BE SENDING HOME NOTES TO ALL YOUR PARENTS. Now get on the bus, all of you."

The lines of children stumped sullenly through the archway, glancing back over their shoulders and muttering.

"Quit it," said a girl, elbowing the boy named Jason. She was slightly taller than the others, with pale hair that fell to her shoulders. "Don't be such a jerk."

She looked at Nettle for a moment, her face open and curious. She smiled and gave a tiny wave.

Then she was gone.

The thumping and bumping and yelling faded.

Deep silence fell, broken only by a hollow *tock, tock, tock*-ing that seemed to come from another room. Late afternoon light slanted through the windows. A wide stairway curved gracefully upward. A thing that Nettle recognized (from a picture in the *Cyclopedia*) as a chandelier hung from the room's high, ornate ceiling.

Doors made of panes of glass opened on a large garden—Nettle could see sunny flowerbeds and tree-shaded paths—enclosed on all sides by high stone walls. Nettle rattled the little brass lever on the doors, but they wouldn't open. She turned and noticed letters written above the archway where the children had been standing: This Way Out.

She went through the archway and down a hall. It opened into another room where two big doors were flanked by tall windows. She tried the doors, but they wouldn't open either. Outside, at the foot of a flight of marble steps, the children were filing toward something big and yellow and boxlike. Black lettering along its side said School District 561. A low, deep rumble came from within.

The children climbed in, jostling and yelling. A door slid shut. Then with a roar, the children were gone.

Nettle looked out at human houses, huge and square, each one standing next to the other in its own patch of short grass. She put her face close to the window and peered first one way then the other, but the street (for so it was, she knew from the pictures in the *Cyclopedia*) seemed to go on and on and on.

chapter nine

"Fool!" screeched Toadflax. She slammed her fist on the table. "Little ninny!"

Bracken gaped at the place where Nettle had been a moment before. "What *happened*?"

"All that magic," groaned Toadflax. "Wasted!"

"Where's Nettle?" cried Bracken. *"What happened?"*

"She's in a city. On the Great River," Toadflax snapped. "And it should have been you. But now . . . Curse the little fool. She'll never find it. Not by herself."

"Find what?" said Bracken through clenched teeth.

"The Door. The Door to the other world, so we can get out of this wretched valley. There's a Safehouse near it. I sent her there."

"She's where?" said Bracken numbly.

"She's in a Safehouse. In a human city."

"You sent Nettle all by herself to a human city?"

"Not on purpose!" Toadflax glared. "You were the one I meant to send. You at least would have had a fighting chance.

Oh, she would have gone along. But not because I thought she'd be much use finding the Door."

"Why couldn't *you* go?" said Bracken, glaring back. "If you want to find this Door so much? You with all your magic, what was stopping you?"

Toadflax laughed. "Me? Go myself? To a Safehouse in a gigantic human city? Child, I am *four hundred years old*! I wouldn't last a minute there, not a minute."

"So you thought you'd send *us*, and instead you sent Nettle all by herself," said Bracken. Her face was pale with anger.

"Listen, you," said Toadflax in a voice like acid. "I gathered more magic than you can ever hope for, with more trouble than you can even imagine, to send you while you were still young enough to resist the Fading. While you still had some chance of finding the Door." She glowered at Bracken. "We had one chance, and now it's gone. Gone." Toadflax stared. "Don't you see? Without that Door we are doomed! That's why your mothers went looking for it. They were still young, but not young enough!"

Bracken felt a sudden chill. "Our mothers! You know what happened to our mothers?"

"Possibly," said Toadflax.

"They went looking for the Door? I thought...I thought they went looking for our fathers."

"They believed your fathers went through the Door." Toadflax sighed impatiently. "So naturally they went looking for it."

"But then the *Fading* got them?" cried Bracken.

"All we know is they never came back." Toadflax shrugged. "Some who lose their powers turn to dust. But others just sink into forgetfulness. They become witches who are not witches. Lost, pitiful creatures. I myself would prefer dust.

And you?" she said suddenly. "Which will you prefer when the humans invade the valley?"

Bracken could not speak.

"You were *both* supposed to touch it, when I told you to," said Toadflax. "When I'd explained everything! But she reached out her silly little hand. Without listening! Without waiting."

"Nettle never listens! Don't you even know that?" yelled Bracken. "And don't call her stupid."

"Pah!" spat Toadflax. They glared at each other, then a change seemed to pass over Toadflax's face. "But wait," she said slowly. "Wait."

She stood up, went to the cupboard, and rummaged for a long time. When she came back, she held a yellowed roll of paper tied with a green ribbon.

She untied the ribbon and spread the paper out on the table.

"A guide to the Safehouses of the new country," someone had written across the top in ink now faded to brown. "You could still get there," said Toadflax. "With this map, you could fly there. And if you hurry, you might still have a chance of finding the Door."

On the eastern edge of the map, there was a scattering of human cities. Boston Town, read one. New Amsterdam, read another. To the west there was a region marked Prairies, then a spine of vaguely drawn mountains. And west of that, there was only blank space on which was written Terra Incognita.

Bracken looked up, frowning.

"You could save Nettle from the Fading," added Toadflax quickly. "She is young, the youngest of all. She can hold out a good long while before it takes her. And the door is somewhere near the Safehouse on the Great River. Very near.

Everyone knows that." She gazed at Bracken with an expression that was perhaps meant to be pleasant. "Look here," she said, running a crooked finger across the map. "Each Safehouse is marked with a lantern. The Safehouse on the Great River is the last of them, the farthest one west. Here."

Toadflax put her finger on a line that wavered down the page somewhat east of the mountains. "This is the Great River, of course. The Safehouse you want is on the northern end of it. Right about, oh, here."

Toadflax shifted her finger back across the map, to the mountains. "We're here, of course. So all you have to do is fly due east and a little north, and you'll hit the Great River, I'm quite sure."

Bracken stared at the map, her heartbeat drumming in her ears.

"What's the matter?" asked Toadflax. "Surely, you don't want to let your cousin die?"

"Stop it," said Bracken. She put her face in her hands.

"I know you do not like me, but think about this. *You are our very last chance.* Look up, child," Toadflax said. "Look here." She stretched her hands toward Bracken, and between them appeared a necklace of bone and beads and mother-of-pearl, glinting in the lantern light. "Woodfolk made them," said Toadflax, dangling the necklace.

"Woodfolk beads! You have *Woodfolk beads*!"

"If you go, I'll give them to you. Forever," said Toadflax. "And if you don't go, think of this: Their magic will be lost, gone, swept away with everything else that's ever mattered to you. . . ."

"Stop," said Bracken. "I'm going," she whispered. "I would have gone anyway."

"Splendid," said Toadflax. "Splendid. Now listen. These beads hold a strong enchantment, with one spell to unlock it.

Use them only in dire need, for they will work just three times. No more. And that, too, is only if you use them wisely." She fastened the beads around Bracken's neck and whispered the spell in her ear. "You understand," she said intently. *"Three times only, if your wishes are wise."*

Bracken nodded.

"You must leave quickly. Now, before the others find out." Toadflax strode toward the door.

"But . . ." It seemed so terrible to leave them all—Aunt Iris and Rose and everybody—without saying a word.

"Don't be a fool," snapped Toadflax, seeing her face. "You can't *tell* them. You know they would never let you go. You have journey bread with you? Apples?"

"Yes," said Bracken, dazed. (She always kept some in her pocket.) Slowly, she followed Toadflax out the door and down the rock path.

They stopped at the brink of the ledge and gazed out over the valley. "Look there," Toadflax said suddenly, pointing.

On the moonlit slopes that led up to the pass, dim shapes were flowing, fluid as water. Then as Bracken watched, they slipped back into the trees.

"The wolves are out," said Toadflax. "A good omen." She mounted her broomstick. "Follow me."

They landed near the trees. "Quiet now," said Toadflax. "And don't stare. Wolves don't like being stared at."

A minute later, six dark forms slipped out of the forest, their ears pricked forward. Six pairs of yellow eyes gleamed.

"The Veil . . ." said the largest wolf.

"Ruined," said Toadflax.

"Ah," said the wolf, nodding slowly. "A pity. A great pity. This valley has been a good sanctuary for us. From their guns. Their traps."

"Our kind and your kind have always been allies," said Toadflax. "This witchling is going on a journey. We ask for your help."

The wolf glanced at Bracken, then away into the distance. "Granted."

"Guide her to the edge of the territory you know," said Toadflax. "The eastern edge."

"The eastern edge?" said a third wolf, one with a graying muzzle. "But that is where the settled lands begin. The human world." He paused, puzzled. "You would send one so young alone to the human world?"

"It's the only way. There is no other hope for us," said Toadflax.

"These are dark days indeed," said the first wolf.

"Indeed," said Toadflax shortly. "Merry part," she said to Bracken. "I wish you well. I mean that." A waver in the air, and she was gone.

The biggest wolf nodded at Bracken. For the barest second, she gazed into his slanted yellow eyes. Then with one graceful movement he was off. The other wolves followed, loping in single file. Bracken flew low behind them.

An owl circled above the pass as one by one, the wolves slipped between the rock walls and threaded their way down the boulder-strewn slopes. The gray-muzzled wolf ran last, limping slightly. Eastward, far down the valley, the scattering of small, hard lights shone as brightly as they had the night before. Bracken felt her heart tighten in her chest, but the wolves kept to the high country, far back from the lights.

In time, the wolves climbed a dark ridge, crested its summit, then followed the slopes down and down and down. The air smelled drier now, like sage. As the night ended and the sky lightened, the wolves trotted along a canyon, following a sandy creek bed. They halted by a grove of aspen trees.

"Beyond this lie the foothills, then the flatlands begin," said the biggest wolf. "We wish you luck, witchling."

"Take care," said the gray-muzzled wolf. "Watch for traps."

The pack turned as one and loped back up the canyon.

Bracken tied her hammock in the very center of the aspen grove and climbed in, exhausted. Above her, aspen leaves fluttered against the early morning sky. She set her hat down over her face, but now, in the way that sometimes happens when you are very, very tired, sleep would not come. She scrunched her eyes so tight that colors floated, and then, in the picture-dreams that come just before you go to sleep, Toadflax's face appeared. She was looking straight at Bracken, but it was impossible to tell what she was thinking.

chapter ten

On the very top floor of the human house, Nettle stood at a small dusty window, her face pressed close to the glass. The rows of houses seemed to spread to the end of the world. No mountains rose behind them.

She turned and ran back down the hall. She found another room, another window, but there were no mountains. She ran to another room, then another and another until she knew she had looked in every direction. And still there were no mountains.

The sun was low over the housetops now. Maybe when night came, the stars would give her some clue as to where home was. Though Bracken had always been better at stars.... Nettle pushed the thought away.

Below her lay the walled garden, the one she'd seen through the glass doors in the big room. Asters and goldenrod bloomed amid graceful tall grasses. An ancient-looking oak tree spread its branches above a circle of rowan trees laden with their red berries. The long garden beds seemed to be planted with herbs, though from a distance Nettle could not tell what kind. In a far corner, she could see a little stone roof poking above a thicket of hazel bushes.

She leaned her face against the windowpane, trying not to think about home, about Bracken, about anything. But it didn't work.

She thought about Scabiosa and Rose who were always there, steady and comforting. She thought about Aunt Iris, who loved her so in her scatterbrained way, always. She remembered Sedge and Reed with their merry eyes and quiet jokes. She pictured the cosy circle of cottages and her own empty bed, and Bracken there in the sleeping loft alone, and her heart hurt so she could barely stand it.

Then she drifted back down the hall, from room to empty room. She padded softly down the big staircase, around and around on the wide stairs, until she found herself again in the big room with the chandelier. She was looking toward the doors that opened on the garden when she noticed something along one wall.

It was a row of glass-topped, glass-fronted boxes, set on wooden legs. Nettle walked toward them. Inside the boxes were carved stone figures, wooden masks, pottery bowls, and many other strange and intriguing things. Beside each one sat a small white card. Indonesia. Collection of W. A. Atkinson, read one. Papua, New Guinea, read another. Collection of W. A. Atkinson.

Nettle went from one to the next, looking at everything. Then suddenly she stopped.

For there, resting on a soft brown cloth embroidered with oak leaves and acorns, was a stone about the size of a loaf of bread. It was blue-green, veined with deeper green.

A seeking stone, she realized, hardly breathing.

The paper beside the stone read, *Collection of W. A. Atkinson*.

"*What?*" said Nettle, outraged. It was a *witch's* stone. How could it belong to a human?

She raised her finger and shot out a thin blue spark. Then, swiftly, she cut a hole in the glass. The cut circle dropped onto the stone below and shattered into several pieces. Nettle reached in and nudged the broken glass aside. Then she lifted out the seeking stone and slipped it into her pocket. It wasn't stealing, she told herself. Humans had *no right* to a seeking stone. Or to the cloth—the Woodfolk cloth—she thought, snatching it up.

Collection of W. A. Atkinson, indeed!

Near where the stone had been, she noticed a small book bound in faded green leather. There was something about it. . . . She hesitated only an instant before seizing it and slipping it into her pocket. She ran back up the stairs, heart beating hard, floor after floor, until she came to the highest window. She unlatched it, pushed it open, and climbed through onto the steep slate roof.

Darkness lay over the glowing city. It was night, and yet not at all like night at home. The sky was not velvet black, but a dull, bruised purple. The Cat's Highway and all but the very brightest constellations had vanished.

Nettle crept to a chimney and sat down, shaking.

Later—much later—Nettle sometimes wondered what would have happened if she had climbed on her broomstick right then and flown off into the not-dark night.

But instead, she only sat, numbly. The city's roar made a low and sinister drone. Then, below her, something came gliding down the street. It was the girl with the pale hair.

She was riding a little frame set above two whirling wheels. The girl's knees bobbing up and down seemed to make it go. The girl turned sharply and glided up a path that led to the house. The two-wheeled thing stopped. She swung her leg up and over—she was wearing trousers, like a Woodfolk man—and jumped off. Then she pushed the wheeled thing quickly over the grass, hid it in a clump of bushes, and ran toward the front steps.

"Witch? Witch girl?" she called from below. "Are you there?"

Nettle crouched by the chimney. From below came knocking and tapping.

The girl went around to the side of the house and tapped on another window. "Hello?" she called. "Hello?"

Nettle pulled out her broomstick. She stared down, wavering.

The girl walked slowly back to the bushes. She stared up at the house for a moment more. Then she pulled out the wheeled thing. She set it upright and straddled it.

"Wait!" cried Nettle, swooping down.

The girl froze.

"Who are you?" said Nettle, landing.

"Elizabeth! Elizabeth Bowen. And I came to tell you, that kid Jason? I heard him on the bus. He said he's going to bring his friends tomorrow to look for you in the Atkinson House, and he's said he's going to tell his dad to tell the police to go look for you too. And police have dogs, and dogs can smell. So I thought I should tell you. Warn you."

"I'll be gone by morning!" said Nettle. "I have to get home. But the stars are gone, and I can't see the mountains. . . ."

"Can't you just magic yourself home?"

"It's not that simple."

"You could come to my house," said Elizabeth. "You could hide there. My parents wouldn't be able to see you, would they?"

"No," Nettle said slowly.

"It's awesome, I have to say, that grown-ups can't see you. The teachers, they looked *right at you.*" She laughed softly. "I mean, imagine the possibilities."

"Everybody else saw me." Nettle frowned, remembering.

Elizabeth frowned too. "It was terrible, everybody pointing and staring and screaming like that. Stupid! But there's no one at my house but me and my parents. Jason and those others, you'd be safe from them. And the police, and dogs, and everyone."

Nettle bit her lip, hesitating.

"Today, when you came, it was amazing." Elizabeth paused. "I always, like, *read* about magic. You know? And then it happened!"

"I guess I could hide at your house," said Nettle.

Elizabeth smiled widely. "All *right*!" she said. "Follow me. Stay high, though."

Nettle flew behind as Elizabeth glided away, her shadow flickering beneath the lanterns that lit each side of the street. They turned onto a new street, and then another. Each street seemed to be part of a network of many streets, all laid out in squares.

After a time they turned onto a narrower street where the houses were smaller and made of wood instead of stone. Elizabeth stopped and waved Nettle down.

"See that house there? The white one with the green roof and the big evergreen right next to it? That's my house. My room is on the second floor, in the back there. Behind, see? I'm going to sneak in and, well, I've sort of missed dinner, and I'm going to be in trouble. Which is okay, really! Because they'll just send me to my room. And then I can let you in the window." She looked at Nettle earnestly. "Got that?"

Nettle nodded.

"Okay," said Elizabeth. "Here goes."

Nettle hovered outside Elizabeth's window for what seemed like a long time.

At last a light came on. Elizabeth slid open the window. Nettle ducked and flew through.

"My parents' bedroom is down the hall, so we'll have to be really, really quiet," Elizabeth whispered. "Right now they're still downstairs. They're not too mad, really. So it's okay."

"That's good," whispered Nettle.

Elizabeth watched admiringly as Nettle stowed her broomstick in her pocket. "Cool! Very cool. So, this is my room."

"It's . . . nice," said Nettle, blinking.

Everything seemed to be a very bright color. Pink, purple, yellow, green . . . Heaps of clothing were scattered all over the floor. Books and papers nearly covered the bed.

"Are you tired?" Elizabeth asked. "You look pretty tired." She rummaged underneath the bed. "I have a sleeping bag for when friends stay over, but if my mom comes and it looks like someone's in it and no one's there, she might start wondering. So if you hear anything, get out quick and shove the sleeping bag under the bed, okay? Do you want some pajamas? Or a nightgown?"

"I need to keep my dress on, and my hat right near." Nettle paused. "It's our dresses and hats that make us invisible."

"Okay," said Elizabeth. "The bathroom's down the hall.

I'll show you the way, but be really, really quiet. Did you bring a toothbrush?"

Nettle looked at her blankly.

The sleeping bag was soft and very comfortable. And the bathroom was a wonder: an amazing invention.

Elizabeth shoved a cascade of stuff from the bed and climbed in. "Tomorrow is Saturday," she whispered. *"Yes!"*

"Saturday," said Nettle drowsily, trying to remember what Saturday was. Some kind of human something or other. . . .

And in another moment, she was asleep.

chapter eleven

All day as the sun passed over the aspen grove, Bracken slept uneasily, waking often. Then at last it was night again. She sat up in her hammock.

She ate some of her journey bread and drank a bottle of blackberry juice, then took a last glance around her. The aspen leaves rustled lightly in the night breeze. Already the grove seemed a sheltered place that a part of her—the tight, afraid part—didn't want to leave. But she got on her broomstick anyway. "Go," she told herself and lifted off.

She flew until the snow-topped mountains that had once encircled her world were only a distant glimmer in the moonlight, low on the horizon.

Now on the flatlands, human lights appeared, and some of them moved. *Roar* they went, followed by the silence of the wide night. Then *roar,* silence, and another roar.

Sometimes she passed over long rows of tall poles. The wires that ran between them whined faintly.

Now and then she saw whole clusters of lights, twinkling on the dark plain, and she knew they were human towns.

After what seemed like many, many hours, the night began to fade. Bracken's heart tightened in her chest. She scanned the plain for a hiding place. But the only cover anywhere, the only places to hide in this vast, flat land seemed to be a few scattered clusters of trees.

She flew toward one, slowed, and hovered.

"Who goes there?" said a voice like a wolf's. Then it began to bark.

A dog, Bracken realized. It barked furiously, with mindless hatred. Bracken sped away.

She tried another grove, but there among the trees sat a human house, its windows staring. Another dog bayed. And every moment, the sky grew lighter! Bracken's hand crept to the Woodfolk bead necklace. But Toadflax had told her to use it only in direst need.

Far ahead, a river glittered in the sun's first rays. Bracken sped toward it, then slowed above the cottonwoods that grew along its banks. She landed in a treetop. She stowed her broom but lingered, watching through the screen of leaves as the red sun rose and the sky filled with light.

A bank of clouds lay low in the east, and now, gradually, its underside was lit in brilliant pink, then gold, then orange. "Oh!" breathed Bracken. Sunrise in the mountains was only a glow in the sky—never like this. The distant horizon circled all around. The edge of the sky met the earth.

It seemed, suddenly, that it might be all right to be out in the wide world. Bracken felt brave and strong. She hung her hammock, climbed in and swung gently, hidden by the leaves. She listened to the rush of water and felt the warming sun. She closed her eyes and slept.

* * *

When she woke, the sun had set and night had fallen. She clambered out of her hammock, folded it neatly, and stowed it in her pocket. She had just finished eating and watching the stars come out one by one when she heard the first bark.

She froze, listening.

It was not one dog, but many, she realized with a chill. She got to her feet and pulled her broom from her pocket.

Below her, twigs snapped and a smallish, humpbacked animal came lumbering through the trees. It stood for a moment, its head lolling. Then it staggered to the base of Bracken's tree and began to climb. It had a black mask and a bushy ringed tail. Bracken crouched, watching, as the creature climbed higher. The raccoon, for so it was, crawled along a branch then hunched down, its back to the tree trunk. "Done for," it moaned as the barking grew louder and higher in pitch.

Before Bracken could say anything, a dog bounded through the underbrush, barking in mad excitement. It ran to Bracken's tree, put its two front paws on the trunk and howled into the darkness.

Bracken leapt to her broom as dog after dog ringed the trunk, all baying in triumph.

"Get on!" she cried, hovering in front of the raccoon. His whiskers quivered. Then he jumped. Bracken's broom dipped—he was surprisingly heavy.

The dogs howled frantically. A beam of light raked the tree branches. A dull bang, and something rattled through the leaves.

"Get 'em!" cried a human voice. There was another bang and more rattling. "Get 'em!" the voice cried again.

"That way!" cried the raccoon, amid more banging and

popping. "Yes!" he said gleefully. "My finest escape ever!" More bangs and poppings sounded.

A sudden, searing pain shot through Bracken's leg. The broom lurched wildly.

"That way," gasped the raccoon.

Bracken craned around to see him pointing with one trembling finger.

"There's a farm that way, an old one," he cried. "There's no hunting there."

An owl hooted from a grove. Behind it loomed a swaybacked barn, its hayloft door hanging open. They hurtled through and crashed to the floor. Bracken slid from the broom and lay in a heap, clutching her leg. "You're bleeding," moaned the raccoon, wringing his little hands.

From outside came a crunching, rumbling sound and a tumult of barking.

"It's a pickup truck," gasped the raccoon. "They come in pickup trucks."

Bracken hobbled to the hayloft door and watched, trembling, as two men with guns—*guns!*—got out.

And then a human child—a boy with a gun.

The men and the boy walked up the farmhouse steps and rapped on the door. A light came on above the porch, and the front door opened. "All right, but be quick about it," said a man's voice. The door slammed shut. The dogs barked mindlessly from the pickup truck.

"It came this way!" said the boy's clear voice. "It was *huge.*"

The humans shone lights into the trees, sweeping them in great arcs through the night. Then the boy and one man walked toward the barn.

"Fly!" whispered the raccoon. He grabbed Bracken's broom

and shoved it at her, but when she tried it, everything swirled crazily around her.

"I can't," she moaned.

"This way. Hurry!" said the raccoon, his voice shrill with fear.

Bracken hobbled after him to a far corner where old, dusty hay lay in drifts. She hid herself as best she could. Below them came a sliding, creaking sound.

Two heads emerged through the opening in the hayloft floor and clambered up, guns in hand. "Here," said the man, handing the boy a light. "You find it."

The boy swept the light back and forth along the heavy ceiling beams.

"I told you it was nothing," said the man.

"I saw it," said the boy. "I swear to God I saw it."

The light played around the barn, casting crazy shadows. Then it shone straight into Bracken's eyes.

"A witch!" screamed the boy. He stepped closer. "It's right there! See it?"

"No," said the man.

"Hold the light!" cried the boy. "Shine it right there in the corner." He took his gun in both hands. He was lifting it to his shoulder when Bracken clutched her necklace and whispered the spell.

chapter twelve

The next instant, someone was standing behind the man and the boy. He was an old man, but big and strong-looking.

"What the hell is all this *ruckus*?" he asked. He wasn't carrying a gun.

"It's a witch," cried the boy. "Right there! In the corner! See her?"

"Stop waving that gun around," he said, striding toward Bracken. "It's a little *girl*," he said suddenly. He whirled around. "What the *hell* do you think you two are doing, cornering some little girl?"

"Little girl?" said the other man.

"Get off my place, and never come back. Go!" said the old man, dismissing him with a wave of one big arm. "Get out of here or I'll wrap that gun around your neck."

The man yanked the boy toward him. "Come on," he said, and shoved him toward the trap door. "Move it. This better not be some dumb joke," came the man's voice from below.

"It *wasn't*," said the boy. "I swear. It was a witch."

"Yeah, right," said the man. The voices faded. A door slammed. The pickup truck whined and roared into the night.

Crickets chimed, filling the silence.

"Little girl?" said the old man softly. "Are you there?"

"I'm here," said Bracken. "My leg... I hurt my leg...."

"I'll get a light. I'll be right back," said the man, hurrying down the ladder.

"What *happened*?" asked the raccoon.

"He's a Witchfriend," said Bracken slowly. "This special kind of grownup human who can see witches. I have a magic necklace that called him."

"But is he a *raccoon* friend?" said the raccoon, not moving. "That's the question."

"He won't hurt you. You can come out," said Bracken. But the raccoon stayed in the hay.

A few minutes later the farmer reappeared, a light shining from his hand. He stepped toward her and kneeled down. "Oh my God," he said, shining the light on her leg. "Can you walk?" He helped her up. "Lean on my shoulder. Can you make it down the ladder?"

The farmer went first, then helped Bracken. "My broom..." she said suddenly, but the farmer just scooped her up in his arms and carried her toward the house.

"I've got it," called the raccoon. Bracken heard him scurrying behind.

The farmer pushed the door open with his shoulder and shoved it closed behind him. "Just rest here on the couch. I'll bring the pickup around," he said, setting Bracken down. "We'll get you to the hospital before you know it."

"Wait," said Bracken. A wave of fear swept over her.

"It will be okay," said the farmer. "No one likes the hospital, but you'll be okay." He walked to a low table, picked up a small box with numbers on it, and began jabbing it with his finger.

"No!" said Bracken. "Don't. Please!"

He paused.

"I can't go there. Can't you see? I'm a witch!"

"You're a little girl, wearing a witch costume."

"I cast a spell on you," said Bracken. "That's how you got there so quickly."

"It did seem odd... kind of a *whoosh*, it was." He put a hand to his chin. "You... cast a spell on me?"

Bracken watched him closely, but he didn't seem angry or afraid. "Yes," she said.

"Am I under a spell now?"

"I'm not sure," said Bracken.

He stood lost in thought. "Huh," he said. Then he shook his head and looked again at Bracken's leg. "I'll get a basin," he said. "Soap. Bandages." He hurried into another room, came back, and set things out on a low table next to where Bracken lay. "I was in the army once," said the farmer, washing away the blood. The space between Bracken's knee and ankle was punctured by several angry holes. "I've seen worse. I can dig these out for you."

Bracken swallowed, then nodded.

"Don't watch," said the farmer, and Bracken closed her eyes. "In the army people drink whiskey for pain, but I don't have any whiskey. Saw enough of the stuff in those days to last me a lifetime, I tell you." He worked swiftly, talking all the while in a low, steady voice. "You can open your eyes now."

"They're all out," he said, showing her the little gray balls in the palm of his hand. "Lead shot," he muttered as he pressed a white square of something to Bracken's leg. "If I'd known, I *would* have wrapped that gun around his neck."

He wound more white fabric around her leg. "Poison, lead is. Very bad for waterfowl. You look awful pale—must be bad for witches too."

"I couldn't fly. My broom!" cried Bracken suddenly. "It's outside!"

The farmer opened the door, and the raccoon scurried past. "Here," he said, holding out the broom. He gazed warily at the farmer.

"Clever animals, raccoons," said the farmer. "I had one as a pet when I was a kid. Can you ride your broom with that leg of yours?"

"I don't think so," said Bracken miserably.

"You could rest up here."

"I haven't got much *time*," said Bracken. "I have to rescue my cousin. She's in the City on the Great River."

"The City on the Great River," repeated the farmer.

"I have a map," she said. She pulled it from her pocket and spread it out on the floor.

"Little girl, this is one mighty old map." The farmer bent over it, chin in hand. "I know what city that is," he said when she showed him the place. "I could give you a ride if you want."

"Would you?"

"Sure," he said.

"This cousin of yours," said the farmer as the pickup truck rattled and bumped down the road. The raccoon sat between him and Bracken, watching intently out the windows. "Do you have a plan for rescuing her?"

Bracken swallowed. "No. It's complicated." Her leg throbbed. "It's a long story."

"We've got time," said the farmer, whose name turned out to be Ben.

Bracken told him everything.

"The Safehouse, even if it's still there, it's not going to be easy to find it," he said when she was done. The road was smoother now, and they were beginning to pass through clusters of human houses. "A real city is way, way bigger than these little farm towns."

"These are *little* towns?" asked Bracken.

"Compared to a city? The ones out here are nothing," said Ben.

"Nothing," whispered Bracken.

The dark countryside rolled by. They passed lights and buildings and signs that glowed, and giant hulking towers. "Grain elevators," said Ben when Bracken asked. He glanced at her. "You don't seem to know much about the modern world."

"Witches don't live in the modern world."

"Oh?" said Ben. "And where do they live?"

So Bracken told him about the village. The raccoon listened too, adding a question now and then.

"It almost seems like that raccoon is talking to you sometimes," said the farmer. So Bracken explained about the Language, and how humans couldn't hear it, but witches could.

"Hmm," he said, looking harder at the raccoon. "Interesting."

"It seems strange that you don't know more about witches," said Bracken.

"Why should I know anything about witches?" said the farmer. "I'm just an old corn farmer."

"Because, well, you're a Witchfriend. Witchfriends are this special kind of human grownup who can see witches," she added quickly. "Most grownup humans can't see us at all. Only human children and Witchfriends can. So if you can see us, it means you're our friend."

"That's nice," said Ben, nodding. "Glad to hear it." He

thought for a minute. "I must have been a Witchfriend all my life without knowing it. Because how would you know, if you never got a chance to see witches, that you were their friend? I mean, you're all off hidden away."

"We didn't used to be," said Bracken. "We used to live in the human world, but it was a long time ago." And she explained about that.

Ben listened carefully.

When it was very, very late, the raccoon curled up and went to sleep. The farmer reached forward and touched something. Music and voices filled the dark.

Outside the window, the moon had risen. It was nearly full, and now as Bracken gazed up at it, it seemed to be following along beside her as they sped through the night. It was the same moon that shone in her sleeping loft window.

But here it seemed like a strange moon, a different moon.

chapter thirteen

Nettle sat up in the sleeping bag. Elizabeth was still asleep, sprawled on her back with the quilt under her armpits. Outside it was gray and starting to rain. For a minute Nettle watched the drops slide down the window glass. Then suddenly she remembered the seeking stone and pulled it from her pocket. She touched the stone's cold surface and tried to remember a spell that might work.

Nothing happened.

She remembered the Woodfolk cloth and pulled it out. She ran her fingers over the soft cloth, the smooth stiches, and thought about Woodfolk with a fierce stab of longing. After a long time, she wrapped the stone in the cloth and slipped it back in her pocket, but as she did her hand touched something else. She pulled it out. It was the book she'd found next to the stone in the glass case. The word *Journal* was embossed on the battered leather cover.

She wondered now why she'd taken some old musty-looking diary, but she opened it anyway.

Sickle Moon, read the first page. The faded handwriting was small and quick and plain.

It was wretchedly hot today, and in my human clothes I could barely breathe. I refuse *to wear a corset, but there's no avoiding the tight-waisted dress, the petticoats, the hat that must be fastened to your piled hair with a long, sharp pin. Worst of all are the boots.*

I keep my own precious dress in a satchel tucked tight beneath my arm. My broomstick and hat and seeking stone are safe in the pocket.

Nettle's eyes widened.

Broomstick?

Seeking stone?

A *witch's* diary. Nettle read on.

The city is much, much bigger than I ever could have imagined. There is an incessant din of riverboats hooting, carriages rattling, hammers pounding, men shouting.

My first step must be to find a Witchfriend.

Nettle glanced at Elizabeth, still hard asleep.

It was simple to tell if a grownup human was a Witchfriend—she (or he) could see you. It was different with a human child. But Elizabeth was a Witchfriend, surely?

Nettle bent again over the book.

Quarter Moon, it said.

Yesterday in the early morning I saw a gentle old man. Something about him made me think... perhaps he's a Witchfriend? Though I have been deceived before. I followed him to a bookshop.

I watched through the front window as he took off his hat and coat and hung them on a hook. He walked among the shelves, pausing sometimes to take out a volume or to run his hand along the spines.

How can you tell whether a human is a Witchfriend? It's a brightness in the eyes, yes, but more than that. An openness. An eagerness. An abiding interest in life in all its many forms.

After a time he caught sight of me through the window and nodded in greeting.

A bell rang when I entered. He smiled, his eyes bright and sharp.

Waxing Moon

The bookseller's name is Mr. James. Today I bought a book from him, a volume of poetry. "What an amazing thing a poem is! Like a spell, but not a spell," I said, and watched him closely.

"Quite so," he said pleasantly.

Half-Moon

The bookseller has a daughter named Phoebe who also works in the shop. She wears a gray dress and a black shawl and reminds me of the bird of that name. I wonder if she too might be a Witchfriend, as it often runs in families.

Yesterday they invited me to go with them on a visit. Someone wished to meet me, they said.

We rode on a streetcar and alighted by a grand stone house with towers and turrets, almost like a castle in the Old Country. A servant led us through an entranceway, then into a great, high-ceilinged room and down a passageway to a parlor where an old man—old for a human, at least—was waiting. He rose from his chair and bowed. His name, he told me, was Walter Allan Atkinson.

It was the name on the little white cards.

W. A. Atkinson.

The man who had taken the seeking stone!

Nettle felt a chill. She read on, faster.

Mr. Atkinson looked at me for the briefest moment, then the three humans exchanged a glance.

"We are Witchfriends, all," said Phoebe.

I kept silence, for one cannot be too cautious.

"If you want to be sure of us, we can make a test," Phoebe said gently. "We will leave you alone to put on your witch garb. We will wait in a room just down the hall. Come when you are ready. Then, if you are not invisible to us, you will know that we are telling the truth."

I listened to their footsteps tap away down the hall.

Then I unlaced my boots and kicked them off, gladly. I took off my hat and let my braid fall free. I unbuttoned all the tiny buttons and stepped out of my human dress and bothersome petticoats. What a mountain they made on the floor!

I put on my own true dress and hat and stole down

the hall. I could feel the swing of my braid and the cool, polished floors beneath my toes.

The door at the end of the hall was ajar, and through it I heard their voices. I stood for a moment, then stole silently into the room. I watched them for a minute more before Phoebe glanced up.

"Why, you look lovely," she said.

They came toward me, smiling broadly. "I knew it," said Mr. James to Mr. Atkinson. Mr. Atkinson bowed low. "Merry meet."

I bowed back. "Merry meet, indeed."

Heart's Moon

Mr. Atkinson's house is a Safehouse: a secret haven for witches.

For it happens that in this city on the Great River, the friends and allies of witches are so numerous that they have formed a Secret Society. They study our ways and write down all they can discover. Whether it is accurate or merely human imaginings I have no way of knowing, but Mr. Atkinson has a library of many volumes of witchlore.

The garden here is planted with enchanter's nightshade and heartsease and many other plants that Witchfriends know provide aid and comfort to our kind. In its center grows an oak ringed by a circle of rowan trees. When Phoebe visits, we sit under the oak and talk.

The cook and the butler and the housemaids cannot see me, but the under-housemaid can. She's become the newest member of the Secret Society.

This morning I worked up the courage to ask Mr. Atkinson whether he knew anything of a Door to another world. I explained that I had come to the city to search for it. I told him of the old stories and the Woodfolk tales of a Door that led to a world without humans. I told him then about my dream, the vision I had that the Door would be found in a city, this city. I told him I had dreamed too that it would be near a place of safety, a refuge of some kind.

He asked many questions, and he tells me he will inquire among all the Witchfriends in the Secret Society. He knows every owner of every Safehouse east of the Great River.

Both of us, now, have begun to search for clues in his library. I hardly sleep. I read by day, and at night as well, even when all the lights are dark. Sometimes when I look out the high-arched windows, I see the changing face of the moon.

Phoebe grows more anxious all the time, for she has heard of the Fading, though many in the Society dismiss it as a rumor.

Nettle hunched over the book, reading as fast as she could.

Full Moon

There is magic here, I feel it.

But how will it be revealed? The question gnaws at my very being.

Waning Moon

A troubling thing, a fearful thing: at first I thought I was only imagining it, but for several days now, my pocket has seemed oddly heavy. Then this afternoon in the garden, the sheen of my dress seemed the tiniest bit dulled. And tonight when I tried to light the fire in the library, my fingerspark seemed to sputter for an instant before it caught.

Phoebe is sure it is the Fading. She urges me to leave while I still can.

But I feel in my heart that I still have time. And the Door is so near! I feel it calling me. If I can find it, there will be no need for any of us to live hidden and cowering. We can go to a new world where we can live in freedom and happiness.

Where we will have a future.

Half-Moon

Tonight when I tried to light the fire, my fingerspark shone only the weakest blue, then guttered out. Every hour it is worse. My dull, gray dress hangs on me. My bones ache. I hear a whining sound, like a mosquito inside my head.

The broom in my hand is lifeless. It is only wood and twigs now, nothing more. I will never open my seeking stone again.

Soon I will become a witch who is not a witch. A shell of a being. A shadow. Or maybe I will turn to dust. Perhaps that will be my fate.

I have asked the Society to safeguard this journal, but I have cast a spell on it—my last ever—to hide its true content from human eyes. So you now, who are reading this—you must be a witch, or you would not be able to see these words, the true words, hidden from all humans.

I pray that you are young and strong and can last long enough to find the Door! It is very near. And you must find it. You must, or all of witchkind will share the fate that will soon be mine. To become a witch who is not a witch.

A shade, a shadow.

Be strong, and may Gaia speed you.

Epigaea R

The rest of the pages were blank.

"What's wrong?" said Elizabeth. She was sitting up in bed. "You've been reading for the longest time, all hunched over. Nettle?"

"I found this book," said Nettle slowly. "And it's a witch's diary. And this witch, she came to this city, and she stayed in that big house, that same house where I was."

"The Atkinson House?"

"Yes. She was looking for a door. The Door to another world."

"At the *Atkinson* House?"

"Yes. Or nearby."

"And . . . you found her diary?"

"In the Atkinson House. In a glass case."

"Wait. You *stole* it?"

"It's a witch's book! It didn't belong to humans."

"But you took it from a glass case? Did you break the glass?"

"I cut a hole in it."

"Whoa," said Elizabeth softly. "At least you didn't get caught. But you'd better stay away from the Atkinson House, is all I can say."

"But I can't!" cried Nettle. "I have to find the Door!"

"But Nettle . . ." Elizabeth broke off, listening.

"Elizabeth?" said a voice. A knock sounded on the door. "Elizabeth?"

Nettle slipped from the sleeping bag and shoved it under the bed just before the door opened.

"Can I come in?" said a woman, peering into the room. "I thought I heard voices. Elizabeth, it's ten o'clock in the morning!"

The woman standing in the doorway had Elizabeth's pale hair and gray-blue eyes and open face. She was Elizabeth's mother; Nettle could tell instantly. Nettle could barely breathe, she felt such longing looking at the two of them, mother and daughter, together.

"Sweetie, are you sick or something?" said Elizabeth's mother. She stepped forward and felt Elizabeth's forehead. "Why are you just sitting there in your pajamas?"

"I've been, well, thinking a lot," said Elizabeth. "Trying to figure some things out."

"Well, get dressed and have breakfast," said her mother. "We thought since it's raining we'd go to the art museum."

"That's okay," said Elizabeth. "I think I'll just read."

"What if we went to the movies?"

"I've got things to do. Stuff. You know."

Her mother sighed. "We'll be back by afternoon. And you haven't been to the museum in ages."

"That's okay, Mom."

"Are you going over to Alice's house?"

"Alice is gone on a trip. Remember?"

"Well, all right," said her mother. "There's oatmeal. I made oatmeal. Leave a note if you go anywhere, and *this time* be home for dinner. Got that?"

"Right," said Elizabeth.

The door closed.

They watched from Elizabeth's parents' bedroom window as the car rolled down the street and away.

"A door?" asked Elizabeth. "You really think there's a door to another world?"

"All I know is what I read in the diary. And it said if you are reading this, it's up to you to find the Door to another world."

Elizabeth frowned. "*Now* what are you going to do?"

"Go to the Atkinson House. Look for the Door."

"You can't go! Not today! Remember? Jason and those other kids will be looking for you."

"I'll go tonight then," said Nettle.

Elizabeth nodded slowly. "Tonight." She brightened. "But anyway, now we have today at least. Come on downstairs."

It was funny, really, how that day with Elizabeth stuck out in Nettle's mind forever after.

They walked around her house and looked at everything. They went to the kitchen, which was full of strange inventions: a humming box, and things that dinged, and a stove that made flames with a click and a whoosh. They sat at the kitchen table and ate strange human food. But most of all, they talked.

Elizabeth told Nettle about school, and the kids at school, and Nettle had lots and lots of questions. "Don't witches go to school?" Elizabeth asked finally.

"We have lessons with Rose," said Nettle.

"Magic lessons?"

"Yes."

Elizabeth sighed. "I am *so* envious, I cannot tell you how envious I am."

They talked about their families: Elizabeth's mother and father and aunts and uncles and cousins. . . .

Then Nettle told Elizabeth about Bracken and how the two of them were cousins and lived with Great-Aunt Iris. "The others in the village, Rose and everyone—well, everyone except this one witch—they all live close. In this little circle of cottages. We can all see each other's front porches."

Elizabeth hesitated. "What about your parents?" she asked quietly.

Nettle looked away. "Our mothers are gone, and our fathers too. They disappeared. And our grandmother died of sorrow, and Aunt Iris took us to live with her. I was only a baby, and Bracken was really little."

"That's awful," said Elizabeth. She bit her lip, frowning. "But your parents. . . . Nettle? What happened to them?"

"No one in the village would ever say. But now . . . I think now they went into the other world."

"You really think so?"

Nettle nodded slowly. "Yes."

Elizabeth frowned. "So, you think they just left you and your cousin behind?"

"No! I think something must have happened. Because they never would. Not on purpose."

A silence, then Nettle said, "I think if I find the Door, I might be able to see them again."

"Oh," said Elizabeth softly.

"Maybe there are clues in the diary," Elizabeth said after a while.

Nettle pulled out the diary and handed it to her.

"A Natural History of Witches," Elizabeth read aloud. *"A Field Guide to the Habits, Customs, and Culture of the Various and Sundry Folk Known..."* She looked up. "This isn't a diary."

"Huh," said Nettle "There must be different words when humans read it."

Elizabeth turned the page. "There might be clues here!" She flipped forward, scanning the pages.

"Read it out *loud,*" said Nettle.

It was all about witches. "Wow," Elizabeth kept saying, looking up from the pages.

But nothing seemed to lead to the Door.

Then Nettle read the diary aloud to Elizabeth, with all its hidden-from-humans words.

But still, nothing seemed like a clue to the Door, or maybe everything was and the key was to sort it all out, but all it did was make Nettle's head hurt.

They talked then about whether Elizabeth should come too, when Nettle went to the Safehouse that night. But in the end, they decided Elizabeth could be seen, and that would put Nettle in danger. So however much Elizabeth wanted to ride a broomstick, she wouldn't. They decided Nettle should wait until late, when for sure there would be no one inside the Atkinson House.

They were in the kitchen eating something called peanut butter sandwiches when Elizabeth's parents came home—Elizabeth heard the car in the driveway. Nettle ran upstairs to Elizabeth's room.

Later Elizabeth came up and they read her books—she had wonderful ones—until suppertime. After supper Elizabeth brought Nettle some smuggled food and they read some more, but it was hard to concentrate on anything. And then at last it was late; Elizabeth's mother came to say good-night and then went away again.

"Good luck," said Elizabeth gravely as Nettle pulled out her broomstick. "You know the way, right?"

"To the Atkinson House? Yes," said Nettle.

"I mean here too. 721 Elm Street. In case you need to come back."

Nettle nodded.

"Good-bye then," said Elizabeth sadly. She opened the window wide.

Nettle bowed. "Fare-thee-well and merry be." She paused awkwardly, then suddenly pulled the diary—*A Natural History of Witches*—from her pocket and handed it to Elizabeth. "Here," she said. "You can keep it. And thank you for helping me."

chapter fourteen

The rain fell steadily, sloshing in rivers down the front window of the pickup truck.

A sort of blade moved back and forth across the window, swishing off the water with a steady *thwak, thwak, thwak.*

Bracken glanced at the farmer, but he didn't seem tired.

"Aren't you going to need to sleep sometime?" she asked at last.

Ben shrugged. "It's kind of strange. I think it's the spell, but I don't feel tired at all."

In the middle of the morning they stopped at a place called Gordie's Econo-Mart. The farmer came back with a large brown bag, a jug of water, and a little dish. "For the coon," he said. "So he can wash his food before he eats it. They do that, you know. I bought him some sweet corn too."

He set the things in back, then steered the truck along a dirt road past a sign that said WAYSIDE REST. It turned out to be a clump of trees and some rickety wooden tables, each with a roof over the top. Raindrops splattered on the roofs and blew in on the tables.

"We'll reach the city by tonight for sure," said Ben after they had eaten. "It will be a miracle if we find the Safehouse, though. I mean, I'm happy to try. But it really sounds like a long shot to me." He shook his head. "A very long shot."

"How's your leg?" asked the raccoon.

"Not very good," admitted Bracken.

"Can you fly yet?"

Bracken stood up and pulled out her broomstick. She climbed on and stood poised, her leg throbbing terribly. Raindrops tapped her hat brim.

"Well?" said the raccoon.

"I can't," gasped Bracken. "Nothing happens."

Slowly, Bracken put her broom in her pocket and sat back down.

"It's got to be the lead," said Ben.

The rain beat harder.

chapter fifteen

To think about looking for the Door was one thing, but where did you start? Nettle leaned over her broomstick, hovering uncertainly above the Atkinson House.

Something wafted toward her. A scent, a hint of spun spell. . . . It was coming from the walled garden around the great oak.

She skimmed the tree's huge crown and landed on grass still wet from the long rain. She walked along the flowerbeds, sniffing. They were planted with many types of herbs, but none of them gave off the mysterious scent. She spotted a patch of enchanter's nightshade: a plant small and modest, but powerful. As she crouched down and breathed in, the roar of the city seemed to fade away.

Then a hand touched her shoulder.

Nettle jumped and spun around.

It was an old, messy-haired woman. She wore trousers and big muddy boots and spectacles that glinted in the harsh not-dark of the city. But she could see Nettle, obviously. "Did the nightshade bring you?" she asked.

"Yes," said Nettle, startled.

"So it's worked! Old Mr. Atkinson would be very pleased."

"What?" said Nettle, staring.

"Mr. Atkinson liked witches. He put it in his will that there would always be a garden here with the sorts of plants that witches like. The rowan trees, the nightshade. That big oak. He'd be pleased to know it finally worked."

"Who *are* you?" asked Nettle.

"My name's Dee," said the woman. "I'm the gardener here. I've come to weed the nightshade. By moonlight, when it sends out its scent," she added, prodding the plants with her walking stick. "But *you* should keep an eye out." She nodded wisely. "The police have been around. Somebody took some very witchy items from the glass cases in the big house," she said, looking hard at Nettle.

"They didn't belong to humans," said Nettle.

"No," agreed the woman. "I don't suppose they did. Or to Mr. Atkinson, either."

"Did you know him?" asked Nettle.

"I'm not *that* old! But I've read about him. I've worked here a long time. The Atkinson House has a whole library of books about witches, did you know that? Though some don't want to admit that now." She laughed. " 'Special Collections,' they call them, but they're all still there if you know what to ask for. And I've read them all."

"Did you ever hear of the Door?" blurted Nettle. "There's supposed to be a door somewhere here, a door to another world."

The woman thought for a long time. "Door," she muttered. "Door. . . . It seems to me there *was* something about a door."

She leaned on her walking stick, frowning. She bit her thumbnail and tapped her foot. "Maybe my sister will know," she said at last. "Come."

"People used to say old Mr. Atkinson was a crackpot, but *I* never believed it," she said as she stumped down the path. They followed it to a patch of hazel bushes growing in a far corner of the garden. "The potting shed," she said, waving her walking stick. "They made it into a gardener's house."

"Anna!" she called, kicking off her boots and banging open the door. "Anna! Do you remember anything about a hidden door in the big house?"

It was a messy and crowded room, filled with old bottles and empty cans and piles of magazines stacked high against the walls. "No," said a woman sitting in the gloom.

"I found a witch in the garden!"

"Witches are dead and gone. Dead. And. Gone."

"That's what you think," said Dee. "Look, here's one. The nightshade called her in! Come, turn the lights on. It's no use sitting in the dark."

"I can't find the extension cord," said Anna.

"It's around here someplace," said Dee. She reached down and rummaged, then suddenly a light came on. It was a little milky globe, dangling from the ceiling by a single cord. "Fire up the hot plate, Anna. We'll make some tea."

It was odd, sitting in the little house. The walls were the familiar gray stone of home. The windows had many small, wavering panes, just like the ones in a witch's cottage. The tea tasted almost like meadow-mint. But other things were a mystery. Nettle's teacup had writing on it that said Dunkin' Donuts. Anna's said Have a Nice Day. "Thrift shops," said Anna, as though that explained anything.

Nettle leaned over her tea and breathed in the steam, for

that was what you did with tea, to be polite and to honor the plants that were giving up their essence. She looked up—Dee and Anna were doing the same thing. Both their spectacles filled with fog. They took them off and set them on the table, and it was then that Nettle noticed that their eyes were a deep violet-blue.

They had once been *witches*, she realized with a shock. Oh, it was awful to think of! And the Fading must have taken away their powers.

"Dee," she said cautiously. "Anna. Were you once... witches?"

"Witches?" Dee shook her head. "How could *we* be witches?" asked Anna.

"I think you were," said Nettle urgently. "And then, well, I think something called the Fading got you. Did you ever hear of the Fading?"

Anna frowned. "No."

Dee shook her head again.

Then all of a sudden a thought struck Nettle.

It was an *awful* thought, a terrible thought—so awful that she couldn't stop staring at the two old women who sat across the table from her.

Dee.

Nettle's mother's name was A*de*lia.

"Dee," said Nettle. "Is your full name Adelia?"

Dee looked puzzled. "It might be. I've forgotten, really."

Nettle asked Anna, "Was your name Nicotiana?" Because that was Bracken's mother's name.

Anna frowned. "I think it *might* have been," she said slowly. "But no one calls me that anymore."

"Where did you come from?" asked Nettle, her heart sinking.

"We don't know," said Dee. "That's the thing. We can't remember anything before we came here. Nothing at all."

"We were hired as the gardeners at the Atkinson House. For the witch plants," said Anna. "We knew about herbs. But that's all we remember."

"We've forgotten all of our old lives," said Dee softly. "So many memories that were important to us...They're lost. Gone."

Nettle put her hands to her face and turned away, shaking.

How do you tell someone she is your own lost mother?

And what if the mother you thought you would find someday turns out to be completely different than you imagined? An old not-witch with muddy boots.

Nettle stood for a long time, there in the cluttered cottage with her back to the two old women. Everything was going wrong. Everything.

"Is there something we can help you with?" asked Dee at last, her voice kind.

Nettle took her hands from her face. She stood for a moment, not knowing what to do. Then she turned back.

"The Door," she said, her voice quavering. "Do you remember anything at all about a door?"

"Door," said Anna. "Door."

"There's a door near the Atkinson House. A door to another world. I think maybe it's the reason you came here. I think you were looking for it."

Dee bit her lip. "It does seem to me there might have been a door."

"If Bracken were here, she could do a remembering spell," said Nettle.

"Bracken," said Anna.

Your *daughter!* Nettle almost said, but it was too sad, too terrible. "My cousin," she said instead. "She's better at spells. I never remember them quite right. But I could try to get you to remember. Because I do really, really need to find the Door."

"Try," said Dee.

Breathe, thought Nettle. Breathe, and the spell came back to her.

Most of it, at least.

She let out an impatient breath, *huh,* and began. " 'Rosemary green, and lavender blue, thyme and sweet marjoram, hyssop and rue,' " she muttered. There was more: something, some something. . . . Drat. Still, she made a spark from her finger—the last part of the remembering spell. "Awake, memory," she said and held the light high.

Anna and Dee looked at it, transfixed.

"We came from somewhere else, I know that," said Dee slowly. "Home was someplace far away, and then for some reason we came here."

"Did you find the Door?" cried Nettle. "The Door to another world?"

"It seems to me we might have," said Dee. She shook her head. "But I can't remember."

chapter sixteen

It was night when Bracken and Ben and the raccoon reached the City on the Great River. Lines of cars streamed in front of them, behind them, and on either side. Lights flashed and whizzed. Green signs saying things like Exit 24 came careening out of the glare, hovered above, then vanished as the pickup truck sped underneath.

"I don't like this," muttered the raccoon. He held his tail, fingering it nervously. "I don't like this at all."

Ben leaned over the wheel, his big-knuckled hands gripping it tightly. Every once in a while he muttered something under his breath.

The raccoon turned to Bracken. "How about using that necklace of yours? Just *wish* us to the house and out of this!"

Bracken touched the cool, smooth beads. "It only works three times," she told the raccoon. "It has to be dire need. And it has to be a wise wish."

"Look," said the raccoon. He put his little hand on her

arm. "Wise means not getting killed! Doesn't it? And dire? Believe me, I know dire when I see it."

Bracken shook her head.

"But you would still have one wish left!"

"I just don't think I should," said Bracken.

Three wise wishes.... If you made an unwise one, maybe it wouldn't be granted, and it wouldn't count against your wishes? Or maybe it would, and one of your precious wishes would be wasted?

She was still puzzling and worrying when Ben spoke up.

"I'm guessing this house you're looking for is an old house," he said. "If it was on that map of yours, it's got to be. So it's in the old part of the city. I'm going to try to find the oldest neighborhood, and then maybe something will come to you, huh? I mean, if it's a magic house and all, maybe you'll recognize it, somehow."

"I'll try," said Bracken.

The raccoon sighed heavily.

Ben stopped the pickup truck at what Bracken now knew was a gas station (the farmer had bought gas several times already) and talked for a long time with a man inside. Bracken and the raccoon watched through the big glass windows.

"He's a good human," said the raccoon. "There are some, you know."

"He *is* a good human," said Bracken.

Ben came back. "Guy thought I was kind of nuts," he said, climbing onto the seat and starting the truck. "But I think I know where to go. Sort of."

After a time he swerved from the giant road onto a narrower one. Soon there were fewer gleaming, lighted buildings and fewer cars. "We should hit the river pretty soon," he said. "The guy said there are a lot of old houses along the river."

It took several more gas stations, but at last they found the river. It ran, dark and quiet, at the bottom of a deep and forested gorge. Houses all along it overlooked the river.

"This is a nice, quiet neighborhood," said the farmer. The street was lined with big spreading trees and street lanterns like the ones in the *Cyclopedia*. In the far distance Bracken saw a bridge, its line of lights reflecting in the dark water.

"What do you think of these?" asked Ben. "These houses seem like they were built a long time ago. Do any of these look likely?"

"I don't know what to look for," said Bracken miserably. "I can't think..."

They drove on, past house after house after house.

At last Ben stopped the truck. "I don't think this is going to work."

"Bracken." The raccoon turned his little bandit face to her. "This is dire need."

She looked out over the river, her heart beating hard. The bridge's string of glimmering lights reminded her of a necklace. Perhaps it's an omen, Bracken thought.

She put her hand to her necklace and wished.

At first, nothing seemed to happen. Bracken put her face in her hands.

"Don't cry," said Ben. "Please."

But Bracken *was* crying. There was no other sound in the pickup truck.

"Bracken," said the farmer suddenly. "Wait! I feel something."

Bracken snuffled and stopped.

"I think something *did* happen when you wished. It's like this funny feeling behind my eyes. And it seems like... I think maybe I know where to go," said Ben.

"You do?" said Bracken.

"*Seems* like it."

"Start the truck!" said the raccoon. "The necklace comes through again!"

They drove along the river.

Ben slowed at a corner and paused for a second, then turned onto a street that led away from the river. They turned several more times, Ben pausing before each turn, then they stopped in front of a big castle-like house. The farmer shut off the truck and its noise died away. "Is that it?" he asked.

Bracken rolled down the window. "I don't know. Maybe."

The farmer hurried around and opened the door for her. Bracken got out, and all three walked slowly toward the house.

"That wall," said Bracken, stopping. "What do you suppose is behind it?"

"A garden, I bet," said the farmer. "Big places like this, they have those formal gardens."

"There's magic in that garden," said Bracken. "I can feel it." She hobbled toward the wall, then craned her neck to look up.

It was a very tall wall, all covered with vines. There was a door in the wall but when Ben tried it, it was locked.

"I can climb over and take a look around," said the raccoon. He grabbed on to the vines and pulled himself upward.

Nettle tried the remembering spell again, then held her fingerspark high. "The Door," she whispered, gazing at Dee and Anna in turn. "Oh, please remember!"

"I can't," said Dee. "It's all a fog."

"Try," pleaded Nettle.

Anna shook her head. "It's no use. Everything is gone."

"Look. I'll get some enchanter's nightshade," said Nettle, running to the door. "It might help. It's quite a powerful herb."

She ran down the path and was almost at the nightshade when she saw something moving in the darkness right in front of her.

A small humpbacked animal seemed to be wandering among the flower beds, sniffing at things. At first Nettle thought it might be a dog. But how would a dog get in the garden? And it didn't move quite like a dog.

It peered up, startled. *"Nettle?"* it said. "Are you Nettle? Because your cousin's looking for you. She's on the other side of the wall."

"Where?" cried Nettle, running toward the raccoon.

He pointed with one finger.

She pulled out her broom and soared over the wall.

"Bracken!" she cried. "BRACKEN!" She swooped down and jumped off her broomstick. She hugged her cousin tight. And then she burst into tears. "Bracken, I met—I think I met—our *mothers*! And they're old. The Fading got them. They're not witches anymore at all! They're little old women who've forgotten everything. They don't know who I am, they won't recognize you. . . ."

"Our *mothers? You found our mothers?*"

"I think so. Just now," said Nettle, the tears streaming down her face. "And they don't seem like our mothers at all."

"But . . ."

"They used to be witches. Their names are Dee and Anna. Like Adelia and Nicotiana, don't you see? And they have our eyes. That's how I knew they were witches, from their eyes. I can't do the remembering spell just right, but *you* could. Then they may remember the Door, where the Door is. I'm looking for this Door. This Door—" She stopped suddenly, noticing the human man who stood nearby.

"He's a Witchfriend. His name is Ben," said Bracken quickly. "Magic brought him."

"Merry meet," said Nettle, nodding.

"Where are they?" asked Bracken.

"They're in the garden. Right over the wall."

"The door's locked," said the Witchfriend, Ben. "We tried it."

"Do an unlocking spell!" said Nettle to Bracken. "You know lots of them."

Bracken touched the lock, muttered a few words, and the door swung open. They all hurried through.

"Bracken, what's wrong with your leg?" asked Nettle.

"I was shot. By hunters."

Nettle stopped. *"What?"*

"In the leg. It *hurts.*"

"Wait here!" Nettle ran ahead and snatched up herbs: heals-all and heartsease and a sprig of enchanter's nightshade. "Here! Try these!" she panted.

Bracken undid her bandage and pressed the herbs to her leg.

"Did it work?" asked the Witchfriend.

"I don't think so," said Bracken. She took a few wobbly steps and winced with pain.

"If it hurts to walk, just fly," said Nettle.

"I can't," said Bracken.

For a moment Nettle could not speak. "You can't fly? It's not the Fading, is it? Say it's not the Fading!"

"I don't know! I don't think so!"

"Shoot your spark! Try it."
Bracken did, and it was clear and blue.
"Good," said Nettle, weak with relief.
"I think it's the lead shot," said Ben, the Witchfriend.
"I'm all right," said Bracken weakly. She trudged on.

chapter seventeen

"They *might* not be our mothers," said Nettle as they neared the cottage. She slowed and stopped. Suddenly she hoped fervently that her real mother was someone else, somewhere else.

But Bracken shook her head. "Our mothers went looking for the Door. Toadflax told me. And she said the Door was near the Safehouse. So it makes sense that they would be here. And Toadflax said sometimes the Fading turns you to dust, but other times you just live on, without your magic. Forgetting everything."

"It's awful," said Nettle.

They reached the door and pushed it open.

"This is my cousin," said Nettle quietly. "She can do a remembering spell."

"Goodness," said Dee. She looked at Bracken with surprise. "That nightshade *is* a powerful herb."

"I'm Ben." He nodded at them. "Ben Niskenen. Witch-friend."

"Hello," said the raccoon cautiously. But Nettle could tell that Dee and Anna couldn't hear him.

Bracken looked from one old woman to the other, her face still and anxious. Then she said the remembering spell, said it perfectly. She held up her spark. "Awake, memory."

Anna and Dee trembled.

"We were," said Dee at last. "We *were* witches. Long ago, and we left the valley for something. To search for the Door. The Door to another world."

Bracken nodded, stricken. "Do you remember who we are?" she asked shakily.

"It almost seems as though I've seen you before," said Anna. "Or maybe it was just someone who looked like you."

Bracken closed her eyes.

"What's wrong?" asked Dee.

Nettle looked to Bracken, and each knew the question the other was thinking. Should they tell? For what good, now, could come of it?

Then Bracken shook her head, just slightly. "Nothing," she said quietly. "Not so much, really."

"It's all right," said Nettle.

"The Door," said Bracken. "Tell us everything you know about the Door."

"There's a stone," said Dee slowly. "We brought it with us. I remember that. And I think the stone has something to do with the Door."

"A seeking stone? *I* have a seeking stone!" said Nettle. She pulled Epigaea's stone from her pocket. "It was in the Atkinson house."

"The one you took from the glass case?" Dee shook her head. "I don't think that was it," she said. "I've seen that one for years. The stone I'm thinking of was another stone."

"It hurts to remember," said Anna dully. "But there was something about our stone, I do know that."

"It *was* a stone, but it was one we brought ourselves, when we came. I feel sure," said Dee.

"Where is it now?" said Bracken. "Think! Where would it be?"

"We hid it somewhere," said Dee. "I remember that."

"There was a spell, a hiding spell," said Anna. Tears ran down her cheeks. "It's hidden somewhere."

"Yes," said Dee. "By a spell. I think it was the last one we ever did."

"In the Safehouse? Did you hide it in the Safehouse?" asked Bracken. "Because that would make sense, wouldn't it? That you would hide it there for another witch to find?"

"I would think so," said Dee. She shook her head. "But I really can't remember."

As they soared toward the Atkinson House, Bracken rode behind Nettle, clinging to Nettle's waist. "We can go through there," said Nettle, steering toward a small, gabled window at the very top.

They landed on the sloping roof just below the window. Bracken muttered a spell. Nettle pushed the window and it swung open. They climbed through and stood listening in the silent house.

Then Bracken began to chant a spell for finding hidden things.

They walked slowly down the hallway, Bracken leaning on Nettle and chanting all the while. They walked down another hallway, and another.

"This is an immense house," said Bracken. "And oh, my

leg aches, and my head too! And I think I hear this little whining in my ears."

The Fading, thought Nettle. Her stomach lurched.

"It seems as though it gets worse the longer I chant," said Bracken.

"Let me do it."

So Bracken told Nettle the spell. Nettle listened, harder than she had in her whole life. She ran down the hallway chanting it, her voice high and shrill in her ears.

At the end, in an alcove nearly hidden under the stairs, she saw it. "Bracken, I've found something!" It was a narrow green door and as she watched, it swung open of its own accord. Bracken came half limping, half running.

It was a tiny attic room, with one window through which the city lights glared and glittered. A wooden box sat on the floor.

Nettle darted through and knelt down. "It's in this box. It must be."

Bracken hobbled over and knelt down beside her. They lifted the lid.

"Oh . . ." sighed Bracken, gazing at the stone. Then, quickly, she reached into the box and picked up the stone with both hands. "The cloth," she whispered as she lifted out the stone, for there was a Woodfolk cloth beneath it. "Get the cloth too. We'll wrap it."

Nettle whisked out the cloth and Bracken slipped it under the stone.

"A Woodfolk cloth," breathed Bracken. "So beautiful . . ." She was tucking in the corners when a mist rose from the stone. It curled toward the low ceiling, twisting in the harsh city light.

"So," said a hollow voice. "You found it. You succeeded on your quest." And out of the mist stepped Toadflax.

"Give me that stone," she said. "I know how to use it. You don't." She held out a bony hand and smiled. "I know what you need to know to pass through the Door. To safety, where the Fading will never get you."

Bracken clutched the stone to her chest.

Toadflax snorted. "Don't look like that. I'll take you with me, of course! Both of you. Hurry. I don't have long. Give it to me."

"But what about the others?" said Bracken.

"We can't *all* go," said Toadflax. "Surely you realize that? Those old crones back in the village, there's no way of saving *them*. It would take forever to get the whole lot of them through. Think about it! They'd be dust before they had a chance."

"But you're older than they are," said Nettle.

"Yes, but I'm wiser too. It was I who set everything in motion." Toadflax smiled, horribly. "I who cast the needed spell."

"What spell?" breathed Nettle.

"Why, the one I cast the night the Veil failed. A black but clever one." She smiled again. "The magic that would bring me, instantly, as soon as you found the stone that holds the secret to the Door." She paused, breathing hard. "Now I can get through, and I can take you with me. But we must hurry!"

"You tricked us," said Nettle.

"What does that matter now?" screeched Toadflax. "Take the chance I'm offering you!"

Bracken didn't move.

"Listen to me!" pleaded Toadflax. "Quickly now! We can get through if we hurry. We can succeed where everyone else failed!"

"And leave everybody else behind?" said Nettle. "Our mothers wouldn't have done that."

Toadflax smiled grimly. "Oh, but they would. They were looking for your fathers! *That's* who they cared about."

"You're lying!" cried Nettle. "That isn't true!"

"It is," said Toadflax. "And think about this—your fathers are there, waiting, on the other side of the Door! Don't you want to see them?" She paused, watching them. "I know the way," she said. Her voice was sweeter, coaxing. "All we need is that stone."

"That can't be right," said Bracken. "Our mothers weren't like that."

"The whole world is like that," said Toadflax. "This world is ruined, child," she said softly. "Give me the stone, and I'll take you to a new one. Hurry!" Already the shimmer on her dress was beginning to dull.

"The Fading," said Nettle, staring in horror.

"Hurry!" shrieked Toadflax. "I don't have long! Come," she wheedled. "It was the only way. Don't you see? There's a *new world*, just waiting for you, and all you have to do is give me that stone."

"It's not right, what you say. It can't be," said Nettle.

"Give it to me!" shrieked Toadflax. A spark flared from her finger and shot toward Bracken's chest.

"No," cried Nettle, casting her own spark back.

The two sparks met, snapping and flaring.

Then the spark from Toadflax's finger thinned and grew pale. "Fah!" she spat, as it sputtered and went out. Now her dress was gray as ashes. "Fools," she cried again and sank into dust.

Nettle stared at the glittering pile, breathing hard. "I didn't . . . I didn't mean for her to die."

"The Fading killed her," said Bracken shakily. "Not you." She picked up the Woodfolk cloth where it had fallen and wrapped it around the stone. "She had a bad heart. A selfish heart."

"Bracken," said Nettle suddenly. "Did we do the right thing?"

"We did the right thing," said Bracken miserably. "To go with her, to leave the others behind, it would have been wrong. It would have been evil."

Slowly, Bracken put the stone in her pocket. Nettle walked and Bracken hobbled down the hall to the little window. They climbed through and crouched on the roof. Nettle reached for her broomstick, then stopped, staring down.

Two men, both dressed alike in blue, were walking toward the house.

"The *police*!" said Nettle suddenly. "I think those humans are police!"

"Police?"

"They punish people who steal things."

The men had lights in their hands and were beaming them back and forth. One man's light swept across the garden wall and stopped. The door hung open. The two men walked toward it, shining their lights.

"Bracken," said Nettle, staring down. "Do you think they might think Dee and Anna stole the stone?"

"Or Ben," moaned Bracken. "They might think it was Ben!"

"Humans put people in *prison*! If you take things, and they catch you, they lock you away."

"Fly!" said Bracken. "Hurry."

They swooped down, and even as they landed Bracken was muttering the spell. "Stop!" she cried and at her voice the two men froze, staring right through her.

"Don't move," said Bracken. Her fingers were spread wide, aimed at them. "Calmly, calmly, walk the way." She twirled as best she could and breathed out the spell. "You will tell all the other police humans that there was nothing at all that you noticed tonight," she said. "You have NO IDEA who stole anything, anything at all from this house, and you never will. You and all the other police humans will never, ever catch anybody, and no one will ever be locked away for taking things from this house. Do you understand?"

The men nodded.

"You will forget this ever happened. Now go!" said Bracken, and the two men turned and walked away.

"That was hard," said Bracken, dazed. "Really hard."

"Good for you, though. I'm glad you did it," said Nettle.

Bracken leaned on her shoulder. They staggered into the garden and pulled the door shut behind them.

chapter eighteen

The others were waiting in the little stone house.

"Did you get it?" cried Ben.

"Yes, but it was awful," moaned Nettle. "Awful." She squeezed her eyes tight shut, willing herself not to cry, but still the tears leaked out. "Toadflax came, this terrible witch. And she said she had the magic to find the Door. She said if we didn't come with her, we would never get another chance."

"She said our *fathers* were waiting and it was the only way to find them," said Bracken in a broken voice. "She said all our mothers cared about was them. That our mothers would have gone through the door and just left us behind if the Fading hadn't gotten them first."

Dee patted them both on the shoulders. "Things will be okay," she said awkwardly. "Really they will."

"I'm sure your mothers wouldn't have done that," said Anna. "Don't cry," she said uncomfortably. "Please don't cry."

But they did cry.

Dee and Anna and Ben the Witchfriend and the raccoon all stood around and said kind and comforting things. Ben gave them an oil-stained red bandanna to use as a handkerchief, but nothing seemed to help.

Still, no one can cry forever.

"There now," said Ben, when at last they had stopped.

"And you do have the stone," said Dee. "Maybe you can get to the other world anyway. On your own."

Bracken looked at her in silence. Then she pulled the stone from her pocket. "I wonder," she said slowly. "I wonder . . . if it's as hard to do as Toadflax told us it was? Because if a secret is hidden in the stone, who would have hidden it?"

"Us," said Dee, nodding slowly.

Bracken nodded back. "And you wouldn't have made it a hard spell, would you? Because why would you do that, if you wanted another witch to find it?"

"We wouldn't," said Dee. "We would have made a simple one."

Bracken put her palm on the stone. " 'Open,' " she said.

And there, deep inside it, was the image of the great oak that grew right outside in the garden.

"Can you see?" asked Dee, peering into the stone. "Is there anything there?"

"It's the oak," said Nettle. "The great big oak in the garden."

"But there's no Door *there*," said Dee, frowning. "Is there?"

"I think it takes another spell," said Bracken. She put her hand to her forehead.

"Are you all right?" asked Dee.

"My head hurts," said Bracken. "It hurts more when I do magic. And my leg aches."

The Fading, thought Nettle again. But it would not happen to Bracken.

It couldn't.

Bracken took a breath, then murmured some more, her face pale. Trembling, she passed her hand over the stone.

And deep in the stone, words formed themselves out of mist. **Touch the tree, and say this spell, and the Door shall appear. Enter and welcome, seeker.** Beneath that, in tiny silver lettering, were the words of a very simple spell.

"You did it," said Nettle softly. "Oh, Bracken! You did it!"

"The others at home," said Bracken. "We have to take them through the Door too."

"But how can we?" asked Nettle. "They'll never make it to the oak before the Fading gets them." In her mind she saw a ragged V of witches falling from the city sky, spiraling down in a flutter of black, turning to glittering dust. . . .

"I have Woodfolk beads," said Bracken. "If we can fly home, we can wish everybody back here with the beads. We can magic them right to the Door, then hurry them through before they fade."

"You have *Woodfolk beads*?" said Nettle. She had not noticed them before, but now she felt a stab of longing.

"Toadflax gave them to me. She told me they would give me only three wishes, but there is one wish left."

"They're beautiful." Nettle thought for a minute. "*You* could wish us back, and then give the beads to me. Then *I* could wish us all to the city. With one of my three wishes."

Bracken shook her head. "You might not *get* wishes! Toadflax said three wishes only, three wise wishes. She didn't say you could lend the necklace to other people and just get as many as you want. Magic has rules, you know it does."

"Still, I *might* get wishes of my own." Nettle frowned,

thinking. "But it does seem like too big a chance, to wish ourselves back. It would be awful if we got back to the valley and the necklace wouldn't work because all the wishes were used up."

"I have an idea," said Ben the Witchfriend. "You don't have to fly all the way back, with Bracken not feeling so well. You could ride back with us. In the truck. The raccoon and I could take you all the way to the mountains, even."

"Good idea," said the raccoon, nodding. "Excellent idea."

chapter nineteen

As Ben drove, Nettle and Bracken rode beside him on the bench seat with the raccoon between them.

There wasn't room in the truck for Dee and Anna, so even if they had wanted to go home to the mountains, they couldn't. Nettle thought about them as the city faded and was left behind. "Were we right not to tell them who we are?" she asked Bracken.

"I'm not sure," said Bracken, sighing.

"Do you think a human could go through the Door?"

"I doubt it," said Ben. "Because then your new world would just fill up with humans."

"But Dee and Anna aren't really humans," said Nettle. "If they could get their magic back, they'd be witches again."

"But they *can't* get it back," said Bracken. "That's what's so terrible about the Fading."

They rode for a while in silence. "I wonder how they discovered where the Door was and found the spell to go through," said Nettle. "Do you think we'll ever find out?"

"I doubt it," said Bracken. "I think it's a story we'll never know."

"Some things, you never do find out," said Ben. "Sometimes life is like that."

"At least we know where they are. And that they're still alive," said Bracken.

And that would have to be enough.

When it was almost light Ben stopped at a gas station and bought them both pink t-shirts that said SOUTH DAKOTA across the front. When the truck was on the road again, Nettle and Bracken took off their hats and put them in their pockets, then put on the t-shirts over their dresses.

Bracken wasn't sure if they could be seen, but when a car went by, Nettle waved and the driver waved back, so that answered that. Now Nettle and Bracken could pass for human children—at least for one quick glance at sixty miles an hour they could, Ben said.

After that (and much pleading from Nettle), Ben let them scuttle in and use the restroom at gas stations. They were not to spend time looking at everything, but just scuttle back out again before they hopped in the truck and zoomed away. It was much easier and more interesting than having to squat in the dark or run behind a bush every time. Bracken agreed that bathrooms were indeed a marvelous invention.

Her leg was getting much better.

It was night when they reached Ben's farm. "Spell or no spell, I'm going to sleep for a good long while," said Ben. "We can pack for the mountains in the morning."

Nettle and Bracken slept upstairs on a rickety iron bed in a small, north-facing bedroom; the quilt had a musty smell and there were old, faded flowers on the paper stuck to the walls.

When they woke and went downstairs, it was late morning. Ben was cooking pancakes in the kitchen. The raccoon sat on the floor near his new water dish, watching attentively.

"I like sinks," said Nettle as they did the dishes after breakfast. "I wish *we* had sinks. I'm beginning to think we need to be a lot more inventive."

"I hope things are all right in the valley," said Bracken. "What if a whole lot of humans got in while we were gone?"

"We weren't gone that long." Nettle tried to think how many days it had been and couldn't.

"Still," said Bracken.

"You know," said Ben, putting down his dish towel. "I've been thinking. I had an idea."

At first when he told them, they were quite surprised. It had to do with something called "dynamite." But they both agreed that it seemed like a good plan, if all else failed.

After that Ben loaded down the truck with boxes and blankets and jugs of water and things to eat that came in cans. He put in a bundle with straps, like the one they'd seen on the two humans so long ago. "Rucksack," he said. "I had it in the army." He stowed it very carefully in one corner of the truck bed and told them never to touch it.

They weren't leaving until early the next morning, so Nettle and Bracken had time to explore the house. They looked in closets and drawers and cupboards. Most of the rooms were dusty and cobwebby and empty-feeling—it seemed as though Ben lived mostly in the kitchen and the bedroom next to it.

"Maybe I could call up Elizabeth on your telephone," said Nettle. It looked different from the one at Elizabeth's house. Still, it might work.

"We don't have her number," said Ben.

"She lives at 721 Elm Street," said Nettle, but Ben shook his head. A telephone number was not the same as a house number, it turned out.

"You could write her a letter," Ben said. He found some writing paper and a pen. It was a ballpoint pen: most wonderous. Nettle sat down at the kitchen table and wrote a long letter telling Elizabeth everything that had happened. Ben found a stamp and showed her where it went on the envelope, and how to write the address the way the post office wanted you to.

He even called up the postmistress on the telephone to get the zip code.

"I was gone for a while. . . . um hum," he said into the telephone. "Had a few things to do. I'm going out west for a while now. Hitting the road."

Nettle could hear the little voice answering back.

"Yep," Ben said. "I'm not sure, really. Not for a week or so, anyway. Talk to you later."

After supper they all walked out to the mailbox at the end of the long lane. The pink and gold and orange sunset was spread out against the wide sky. Nettle opened the metal door and put the letter inside. Ben showed her how the flag went up for the mailman.

"You don't even limp at all now," said Nettle to Bracken as they walked back.

"It started to feel better before we even left the city. It started right when I got in the truck," said Bracken.

"That's odd," said Nettle. "Why would that be?"

"It does seem strange," said Ben.

The raccoon padded quickly down the road, head down.

"Try flying," he said when they got back to the grove of trees around the farmhouse. "Go ahead. Just try."

Bracken got out her broom and took a deep breath. She pushed off, wobbled, and made a slow circle around.

"You'll be soaring soon, just you watch," said the raccoon.

"How did you know?" asked Nettle, suddenly curious.

"I made a wish," said the raccoon.

"What?" said Bracken, landing. "You *what*?"

"When I was riding beside you in the truck, I touched the necklace. I wished for your leg to get better so you could fly again. I know I'm not a witch! But I figured, why shouldn't a raccoon get a wish? And what was the harm if it didn't work?"

"But...you could have used up the third wish!" cried Bracken.

"*I* wished it, not you," said the raccoon. "And you need to fly, see? You can't spend the rest of your life not *flying*!"

There was a long pause. "It was nice of you," said Bracken tensely. "But didn't you hear what we *said*? About how magic has rules? The necklace only grants three wishes."

The raccoon looked away, shoulders hunched. "I think you worry too much," he said quietly. "I think the magic is more generous than that. And I was sad, seeing you not be able to fly. I felt..." He stopped, then spoke in a voice almost too low for them to hear. "I felt like it was my fault."

"Don't think that! It wasn't your fault!" said Bracken. She squatted down so their two heads were level with each other. "Don't ever think that!"

The raccoon nodded. "Thanks," he muttered. Then they all walked on together.

"Maybe it wasn't his wish that made your leg feel better," said Nettle that night as Nettle and Bracken lay in bed in the spare room. "Or maybe everybody gets some wishes, not just you."

"But we can't take chances," said Bracken. "I'm not sure exactly how it all works out, but we have to be *wise.* We can't just go wishing this and that."

"He wasn't just wishing this and that. He wanted you to fly again!"

"I know, I know," said Bracken.

The wind moaned and whistled through the eaves of the old house. The loose tin on the barn roof banged back and forth.

"I think Ben's lonely here," said Bracken. "His wife died three and a half years ago, he told me. And he's never been out West, he said. He's glad to be going."

"He's a nice human, Ben," said Nettle. "I get the feeling there are a lot of nice humans, you know?"

"Yes."

"Bracken, have you ever thought, well, that if we make it to the other world, you'll be sorry to leave Ben behind?"

"Yes," said Bracken. "And your friend too. Elizabeth. I think I would have liked her."

The next day, they sat in the truck and rode and rode and *rode.*

When it was dark, Bracken got out and checked the stars and figured out what she thought was the right direction—just a little south but still mostly west—so when they reached the mountains, they would be near the valley.

Day came and then—at last—mountains appeared on the horizon. They were a deep purple-blue, with towering clouds riding low above them. It almost seemed as though the mountains were clouds, and the clouds were mountains.

Bracken looked at them for a long time. "This is the right

direction. The outline of the peaks—that's the way I remember them."

Sometimes as the hours passed, Bracken would brush a finger on the Woodfolk beads, not to wish but just to touch them. Every time she did, Nettle sighed heavily.

"Stop it," said Bracken. "You have a seeking stone, don't you? Don't be greedy."

"Well, you have a seeking stone *and* a necklace," said Nettle.

"*And* I got shot," said Bracken. "You didn't get shot."

"Your leg is fine now," said Nettle, "and you have a raccoon."

"He's not my raccoon," said Bracken.

"Well, he likes you better."

"I *rescued* him," said Bracken.

Which was true, thought Nettle gloomily. But on the other hand, she'd gotten to meet Elizabeth. And remembering that, she felt better.

When they got to the foothills, they followed a dusty gravel road that wound up and up until the sagebrush gave way to tall pines and the air began to smell like home. The road got bumpier. Rocks banged against the bottom of the pickup truck. Soon the truck seemed to make more and more noise in order to get anywhere. Then, finally, it stopped.

"End of the road," said Ben.

He opened what was called the glove compartment, took out some papers, and stuffed them into his pocket. He got out and walked to the front of the truck. He took down the little metal sign with letters and numbers—the license plate, it was called—then walked to the back and removed the other one too. He walked a little way off and hid the license plates under a rock, then returned.

It was all part of Ben's idea, the one they would use if Nettle and Bracken's plan failed.

Nettle and Bracken laid out a hammock between their two broomsticks and tied the ends fast. Ben climbed into the hammock, and the raccoon jumped behind Bracken onto her broomstick. Nettle wished he would ride behind *her*, on *her* broomstick, but she didn't say anything.

"Ready?" asked Bracken.

"I guess so," said Ben, holding tight. "Sure."

They lifted off.

They found their way to the pass with only a few hesitations and wrong turns. They soared through and landed just inside the valley. Ben and the raccoon scrambled to the ground.

Ben stood for a minute gazing out over the valley. Then he and the raccoon sat down with their backs against a rock to wait.

"It will take a while for the coven to decide," Bracken told them. "Witches aren't supposed to have leaders, though Rose is, really. We're supposed to decide things by consensus, which always means a lot of bickering and discussing every last point."

"Good luck," said Ben.

Nettle and Bracken soared down the slopes and over the Least and Middle Meadows. *Home!* Nettle gave a little bounce on her broomstick.

They sped toward the village.

"Look," said Nettle, pointing.

High on the ledge where Toadflax's cottage had stood,

black pointed hats bobbed this way and that among piles of fallen stones.

Scabiosa was the first to look up. "They're back! Oh look, everyone! Look! They're *alive*!" she cried.

"We've found the Door!" said Nettle, landing amid the commotion. "Everybody! *We've found the Door!* The Door to the other world."

"You did?" said Scabiosa in the sudden silence. The others began murmuring and exclaiming.

"Toadflax told us you had gone to look for it," said Rose quietly. "We thought we'd never see you again."

"We went to a city on the Great River and we found it!" said Nettle. "It's in a giant oak near a Safehouse."

"A city," said Rose, looking at them both closely.

"We're fine," said Nettle.

"Bracken?" said Rose.

"I'm all right," said Bracken.

"We think something may have happened to Toadflax," said Rose. "We looked up this morning and her house had fallen down. Her magic is gone. We think she might be . . . dead."

"She is," said Nettle.

Then Bracken told them what had happened.

"She was a fine witch, once," said Scabiosa quietly. "She wasn't always like that, not in the old days before humans grew so powerful. It made her bitter. It ate away her heart."

"There have been three more humans since you left," said Rose. "Two of them got as far as the Middle Meadow."

"They trompled a big path through the meadow," said Violet glumly. "Muddy footprints filled with water."

"But we don't have to worry about it anymore! We can get away. We have *Woodfolk beads*!" said Nettle.

The others looked startled.

"Toadflax gave them to Bracken."

"Toadflax had a Woodfolk necklace!" said Violet. "Why, that *selfish, deceptive...*"

"Never mind that, Violet," said Sedge. "Think what it means, to have Woodfolk beads!"

"We can wish ourselves back to the Door to the other world!" said Nettle. "And we know how to get through! We know the spell. It will only take a minute—we can whisk you right through before you turn to dust. I'm sure we can."

There was a short silence.

"*I'm* not taking a chance on being turned into dust, thank you very much," said Violet.

"But... it's a new world! A new life!" said Nettle.

Nobody said anything.

"Don't you want to go?" asked Nettle.

"It's not the easiest choice in the world," said Scabiosa finally.

"I don't *want* to leave the valley," said a quiet voice. It was Gentian, a kind but timid witch who rarely said anything at the Gathering Fires.

"I don't either," said Penstemmon softly. Penstemmon was another witch who hardly ever said anything and sometimes didn't even come to the Gathering Fires.

"But Gentian! Penstemmon. All of you," said Rose. "Think about it. A whole new world! That's the chance we have."

"I'll go," said Sedge.

"I will," said Reed.

"I won't," said Violet, looking around at the others.

"You would *miss out* on the Door to the other *world*?" said Nettle, incredulous.

Violet frowned. "*You* say there's a door. But you're only a witchling."

Nettle sighed.

* * *

Nothing is ever unanimous among witches.

Aunt Iris, of course, wanted to go so she could be with Nettle and Bracken. And Scabiosa, Rose, Sedge, and Reed were all going.

But Violet, Gentian, and Penstemmon wanted to stay, come what may. "This is our *home,*" said Gentian.

"Penstemmon," pleaded Rose. "Gentian. Violet. There's no *future* for you in this valley! Even if no more humans come, ever, what life will you have here? There will be no more witchlings without Woodfolk. The last of you will grow old, and die, and turn to dust, and that will be the end of it."

"Better dust then than dust now," said Violet.

"*I* would rather die than be the last witch in this world!" said Reed. "There may be *other covens* in the new world! And the Fading! Think of the Fading when the humans come! Surely you don't want to just linger on here, waiting for the end?"

"I don't care," said Penstemmon, looking at the ground. "I'm old and tired and afraid. I want to stay in this valley even if the humans *do* come."

Bracken looked at Nettle.

"Go on," said Nettle. "Tell them."

So Bracken told them about Ben and his idea.

In the shocked silence that followed, Violet had to go sit down on a boulder and fan herself with her hat. "A *human?*" she kept saying in a faint, outraged voice. "*Us*, listen to a human?"

"He's a Witchfriend," said Nettle. "Didn't I say he's a Witchfriend?"

"That doesn't mean he knows what's best for us," said

Violet. "Why, humans hardly live longer than, I don't know. Than *insects*! What do they know about—"

Reed interrupted her. "*I* think it's a good idea."

"So do I," said Sedge.

"I think we should try again on the Veil," said Violet.

"We *have* tried," snapped Rose. "Countless times, as you well know."

More talk, endless talk.

Then at last the stay-in-the-valley ones (except for Violet) agreed that the idea, however strange, *was* worth a try. Aunt Iris still wasn't sure, but the stay-in-the-valley ones insisted that if you were leaving, you didn't get a say, since after all you would be gone soon.

And thus (after *that*, discussion was finally over) it was decided.

"Now, everyone fly to the village, please," said Bracken. "Stay in your cottages until it's safe to come out. And don't argue," she added quickly.

"They actually listened to us, most of them," said Nettle, watching the ragged V of witches fly away. "Amazing."

Nettle and Bracken waited until every witch in the coven was sure to be in her cottage, then flew back to the pass.

"Did they agree to it?" asked Ben.

"Close enough," said Nettle, suddenly nervous.

"All right then," said Ben. "Now *listen carefully.* I'm going to go over the instructions one more time. . . . You understand everything I've said?" he asked when he was done.

"Yes." They both nodded solemnly.

"Do not use your fingersparks at any time! for any reason! Got that?"

"I'm staying here," said the raccoon, wringing his hands.

"Got it?" said Ben again.

"We do understand," said Bracken. "Really."

So with Ben swinging between them, Nettle and Bracken flew high up above the pass and looked for a pattern of deep cracks. They needed a kind of network in the rocks. It didn't take all that long to find them.

They hovered near the first crack. Ben clambered out onto the rock. He waved them off. "Stay back," he said, still waving. "Farther!"

He took a stick of dynamite from his rucksack and then—very carefully—he attached something called a blasting cap. It was small and silver, and it in turn was attached to a long string like a candlewick—a fuse, it was called. When he was done, he stood up, scrambled a little way from the fuse, and waved them back.

After that, they flew him to the next crack.

One by one he set all the sticks into the cliffs above the pass. Each stick's fuse snaked across the rocks to a spot where it connected with all the other fuses, so they could all be lit at once. The place where all the fuses connected was behind a big boulder, far away from the sticks of dynamite.

When all the fuses were connected, they were ready for Ben (and only Ben) to light while taking shelter behind the boulder.

Nettle and Bracken flew high, scanning the slopes for anything that moved. Nettle warned off two hawks and several ravens, who warned the marmots. Soon the news had spread to all the other animals. There was a scurrying and squeaking, then silence.

"All's clear," said Bracken when they had flown back to the boulder.

"Good," said Ben. "Now fly down toward the village.

I'll wait until I'm sure you are far enough away and then some."

"You'll be safe though, won't you?" said Bracken suddenly.

"I've done this in the army," said Ben. "I'll be fine. Now get going, and when you're far enough away I'll signal, just before I light it."

The raccoon climbed on behind Bracken. The three of them flew away until Ben was only a small figure, watching them. They saw him wave widely, which was the signal to put their fingers in their ears. Then he touched the fuses and crouched behind the boulder.

A pause of one beat...

Two beats...

Three beats, and then...

BOOM!

The mountainside began to slide.

Boulders came thundering down, like a thousand games of Catapult all played at once. A great cloud of dust rose.

And when at last silence fell, there was no more pass into the valley.

Ben stood back up and waved.

"It worked," said Ben as soon as Nettle, Bracken, and the raccoon had landed next to him. "Mission accomplished." He seemed very quiet.

They looked down at the valley from what was now the top of an unbroken wall of mountains. It wasn't long before a fluttering black V arose from the village and sped toward what had, until a minute ago, been the pass.

When the witches drew close, they scattered, each witch soaring this way and that over the rubble. Nettle could see them leaning over and muttering.

"I hope they like it," said Ben. "Because there's not a lot we can do if they don't."

"I *did* wonder," said the raccoon. "Dynamite and witches—it seemed like a bad combination."

"*I* think it worked just fine," said Nettle.

Still, none of the witches seemed to be saying anything as they landed.

"Well?" said Nettle.

"It's good," said Scabiosa slowly. "I think it's a good thing. In the balance, anyway."

"But such a mess," said Violet. "Rocks sliding everywhere, everything out of place..."

"Violet," said Penstemmon under her breath. "Show some gratitude." She bowed shyly to Ben. "We thank you, Witchfriend."

"Ben," said Ben, bowing. "Ben Niskenen. It won't work forever, but it ought to hold them off for a while."

"Ben Niskenen, we thank you," said Gentian.

"Well, I'm glad it worked out," said Ben. "Now, well...I think I'd better be getting on back."

"You're going home, then?" said Bracken.

"I think so. I'll need a ride back to the truck, though."

"You're going right now?" said Nettle. She realized suddenly that she hadn't given any thought at all to what Ben would do next.

"I think so," repeated Ben, quietly.

There was an awkward pause.

"Why not stay with us?" said Penstemmon shyly. "You—and the raccoon too—could come live in the valley with us. We'll have plenty of spare cottages when the others leave. You can have your choice."

"That's very nice of you," said Ben, looking startled.

"You have helped us greatly," said Penstemmon. "All of us owe you a great debt."

"It was a good idea, I admit," said Violet grudgingly.

Ben thought for a long moment. "It's nice of you to ask me, it really is. But it doesn't seem right, somehow, for a human to live in a witch village. I think I'd best be getting home."

"But you'll be *lonely*," blurted Nettle.

"Oh, maybe. But there are worse things. I'll miss you," he said to Bracken and Nettle. "It would be nice if you could come home with me, but you can't. That's not the way things are."

The raccoon tugged Bracken's skirt with his little hand. "Tell him *I'll* go home with him."

"Sure," said Ben when Bracken told him. "That would be nice."

So that was the way it was.

Ben climbed into the hammock and waved. Then Bracken and Nettle flew him and the raccoon back to the truck.

No one was there. No humans seemed to have noticed the explosion. So Ben fetched the license plates from under the rock and put them back on the truck.

"I had one more idea," said Ben. "The well on my place, it's very deep. And far from any city. Why don't you take a jug of well water back with you? It *might* work for making a new veil. You never know. I thought you could give it to the ones who are staying behind."

"Good idea," said Nettle.

"They can try," said Bracken, though she seemed doubtful. "Thank you."

Ben took out a jug and set it on the ground. Then he and the raccoon climbed into the truck. "Here goes," said Ben, putting the key in the starting place. The truck made a horrid grinding noise, then another and another.

Bracken went to the window and peered in. "What's wrong?"

Nettle crowded next to her and craned in to see.

"It won't start," Ben said. "I was afraid of that."

"But how will you get home?" said Bracken.

"Oh, we'll manage all right," said Ben, looking worried. "We'll have to, I guess."

"Start, please start," said Nettle to the truck. It roared into life.

"Yikes," said Ben.

Bracken bowed her hat solemnly. "Fare-thee-well and merry be," she said softly. "And thank you, forever."

Ben put his hand to his cap. "So long," he said. "It was good to know you both."

"Good-bye," said the raccoon. "Likewise!"

"Good-bye," said Nettle, bowing. How she hated good-byes!

They watched quietly as the truck rattled its way down the mountain.

"It was strange, how the truck just started right up when you told it too," said Bracken. "It was almost as though..." She stopped dead. "Nettle, could you have been touching the necklace? You were leaning against me! Could you have been touching it by mistake, and then wished the truck would start?"

"Oh..." said Nettle, as the horrible realization of what that might mean sank in.

It seemed as though maybe she might have been touching the necklace. And she'd *so* wanted the truck to start. "I didn't mean to make a wish. Does thinking count for making a wish?"

"I don't know!" said Bracken.

"Try to remember!" said Nettle. "What did Toadflax say, exactly?"

"All she said was three wise wishes. I thought she meant for me, but maybe others could wish too, once the first spell unlocked the necklace. Oh . . ." She put her head in her hands. "It wasn't at all clear! Not at all."

"Of course not," said Nettle bitterly. "Nothing ever was with Toadflax."

Bracken looked sick. "Nettle, *what if all the wishes are used up*?"

chapter twenty

They were flying back to the village when Bracken's leg began to hurt again. "It throbs," she said as they landed on the Commons. She got shakily off her broom.

Rose came down her front steps and hurried over. "What's wrong?" she asked. Scabiosa came running from her cottage.

"My leg," said Bracken. "I was shot by hunters. It seemed completely healed, but now it's starting to hurt again."

"The Fading," gasped Rose. "It could be a symptom of the Fading."

"But it can't be!" said Nettle. "Her spark is still strong."

"Show me," said Rose.

Bracken held up her fingerspark.

"It looks pale," said Scabiosa. "Rose, do you think it looks pale?"

Rose stepped forward and picked up a fold of Bracken's dress. She held it to the sunlight, turning it this way and that. "Has your pocket ever felt heavy?"

"Once," said Bracken. "But it went away. I think I was only imagining it."

"Have you heard a little whining, like a gnat in your ear?" asked Rose.

"Yes," said Bracken. "But it went away. . . ."

"Bracken," said Rose urgently. "Did you do much magic in the city? Because if you did, it would aggravate the Fading. It would sap your strength and make you more vulnerable."

"I did . . . several spells," whispered Bracken.

"Scabiosa, call the others," said Rose. Scabiosa ran, calling out their names.

"Nettle," said Rose. "Did you do spells in the city?"

"Only two," stammered Nettle, "and they didn't work very well. Three," she added, remembering the one in the hall, the one that Bracken had taught her for finding lost things.

"Did any of those things happen to you—the whining, the heavy pocket, the trouble flying?"

"No," said Nettle. "Never."

"Good." Rose nodded grimly. "Now listen. If we are to go, we must go now. And Nettle, you must learn the spell to take us through. Learn it now, so you will be ready the instant we get there."

Trembling, Bracken pulled the stone from her pocket. "It's a simple one."

"Open," said Rose, putting her hand on the stone. "Ah, yes," she said, peering into the stone.

Nettle read the spell. Then she practiced it, whispering it to herself again and again.

"Do you have it?" asked Rose.

"Yes," said Nettle, but she felt sick with dread.

And what if the necklace doesn't work? said a voice in her head. What if the wishes are used up?

There was no time to sing the "Fare-thee-well and merry be and someday maybe we will meet again" song, no time for the parting tears or the one last look around.

"The Fading has begun on Bracken. It's Nettle who must wish us through," said Scabiosa to the terrified circle around them. "Everyone who wants to go, join hands! Now."

Nettle clutched Bracken's hand on one side, Rose's on the other. Aunt Iris and Scabiosa and Reed and Sedge clasped hands. The circle of those who were leaving was complete.

"Fare-thee-well and merry be," said Rose to the rest. "Touch the necklace," she said to Nettle. "Then take my hand again, quick, and wish."

Nettle wished.

There was a long, sickening pause.

"It's not working," moaned Bracken. "The wishes were all gone!"

And then...

The sky and the mountains and all their old life whirled around and around. It was night again, suddenly, for whooshing here and there seemed to do something to time. The stars spun and faded, and the mountain quiet became the low roar of the city.

So the wishes were not all gone, sang a voice in Nettle's head. Then the bitter, magic smell of nightshade hung all around them. They were standing beneath the great oak.

Dee and Anna were waiting. "We've been watching for you," said Dee.

"Oh!" said Nettle, feeling both sad and happy. But there was no time, no time at all! Rose handed her the stone. In a rush of words, she said the very simple spell.

What appeared next, in the oak tree's furrowed trunk, was a black hole, a darkness, a void. But before Nettle had time to be afraid, before she had time to *think*, Rose stepped toward it. She held up her finger, made a spark, and stepped into the darkness.

One horrible second went by. And then, deep in darkness, Rose's spark glimmered.

"Go!" cried Scabiosa, guiding Bracken toward the trunk. Bracken raised her fingerspark, stepped through, and her spark too appeared, strong and blue.

One after another they went through the Door, until only Nettle was left.

chapter twenty-one

"Come with us," she cried to Dee and Anna. "Try!"

Dee pushed her hand against the Door, against the blackness, but her palm stopped in midair as though there was no door, only solid tree trunk. "I can see the Door," she said quietly. "But it's no use. We'll never be witches again. Go now. Hurry."

"Do you know who we are?" blurted Nettle.

Dee's expression softened. "Oh my dear," she said.

"We do, at last," said Anna. "And no matter how it hurts, I'm glad we remembered everything. And we're sorry about what happened."

"It's hard that we were gone so long," said Dee gently. "I wish things had been different. But know this! Even if we'd had magic enough, we wouldn't have gone through the Door without you. We would never go and leave you behind! You know that, don't you?"

"Yes," said Nettle.

"But now you must go through it without us."

"Go!" cried Dee. "Hurry."

Nettle lit her spark. "But I have so many questions! I'll only stay a little—"

"We can't risk it," said Dee. "The Fading is not to be trifled with. Go now. Light your spark! Please."

"We love you," said Anna. "Tell Bracken we loved you both."

"We always did, even when we had forgotten who you were," said Dee. "And we always will."

It was not something a witch would ever say out loud, but it meant everything.

"Oh . . ." said Nettle.

"Go!" said Dee. Gently, she pushed Nettle through.

Nettle felt cool, damp sand beneath her feet. Bracken stood beside her, trembling. They looked back through the door, and for an instant they saw the tiny figures of Dee and Anna and the garden behind them. Then Dee and Anna flickered and vanished, along with all of the human world.

"Wait," moaned Nettle, but there was no going back.

"What happened?" said Rose.

Nettle stood for a moment, dazed. "Oh," she said, not knowing what to say. "Nothing. Everything. . . . I can tell you later."

"Are you all right?"

"It's all right, Rose," said Nettle.

It wasn't really—not then and not ever. But sometimes there is nothing for it but to go on.

Fingersparks shone. Rose, Scabiosa, Aunt Iris, Sedge, and Reed stood around her.

The light flickered on the earthen walls of a tunnel. It was wide and sloped gently upward. A sound washed over them, a distant roaring that rose and fell like the sound of someone breathing. At the end of the tunnel shone a circle of sky, brighter around the edges.

They put out their sparks and walked quietly toward it. They stepped outside. A vast blue opened all around them. Waves crested and broke in white foam. Little, long-legged seabirds skittered across the shining sand, probing it with their slender beaks.

"The ocean!" said Bracken softly. "I've always wanted to see the ocean."

The little birds stopped their probing and circled them on quickly moving legs.

"Welcome," said one.

"We're witches," said Nettle.

"We *know* that," said the first. "We're sandpipers. Pleased to meet you."

"Well, that's settled. Let's go," said one, and the sandpipers skittered toward the waves.

"Wait," said Bracken. "Are there other witches here? And Woodfolk. Are there Woodfolk?"

"Both," said the last of the sandpipers. Their feet left tracks like stitching in the sand.

The waves curled and broke, curled and broke, and wind blew off the ocean.

When Nettle and Bracken turned their backs to the water, they saw windblown, gray-green pines with bare branches like driftwood, high atop pale cliffs that rose from the sand. Beyond the cliffs stood a forest of trees so tall their pointed tops seemed lost in mist.

"Did you hear what they said? Witches and Woodfolk! I like this place," said Nettle.

And Bracken nodded. "I like it too."

In the days that followed, the seven witches built their new village. It took much magic and arguing, but when it was done, the cottages stood high on a cliff top, all in a line. Nettle and Bracken's sleeping loft looked out over the ocean.

Every morning, the two of them went exploring.

They flew low over coves where sea lions arped from the rocks. Seals swam through a forest of seaweed that swayed in the aqua water. Sea otters floated on their backs holding rocks between their front paws, breaking shellfish. The air was filled with the cries of hundreds and hundreds of seabirds nesting on the cliffs.

One day, as they flew over a sweeping half-moon of sand, they saw a path winding up the cliff and into the forest. They landed on the cliff top and followed the path into the woods.

The trees had soft, red trunks. They were so gigantic that when you walked among them, you could see the sunlight on the very tops of the trees and blue patches of sky, but down by the forest floor it was dim, and the air was cool and spicy smelling.

Nettle stopped and pointed. "A fire," she said. They hurried forward.

It was a very small fire, at the base of a particularly large tree. Beside it sat a man. He held a penknife in one nimble hand, a stick of wood in the other. Woodchips flew around him. Nettle and Bracken walked closer, and the Woodfolk man looked up.

"Well now," he said. "Merry meet and merry part." It was hard to tell if he was young or old.

"Are you...Are you from the Quercus tribe?" asked Bracken. For that was their fathers' tribe.

"I'm not," he said. "But I can show you where the gathering camp is." He stood up and slipped his knife into the pocket of his gray-green, raggedy trousers. He glanced at the fire and it went out, leaving not even a burned spot on the forest floor. "Nobody's there now, but all the tribes will be back at midwinter," he said as they set off.

He led them past streams and over hills, striding through the greenish light with a long, loping gait. "Seems to me a tribe of that name came here years ago, through one of the Lesser Passage Trees. Tricky things, those. Lots of people are fooled by them."

Traveling by a Lesser Passage Tree, the Woodfolk man explained, was a risky venture. You might think it was an ordinary Passage Tree, the kind that Woodfolk often took to get from place to place. "But once you step through, you're in another world. And there's no going back."

Bracken looked at Nettle. "So *that's* what happened," she said quietly.

They knew now for certain their fathers hadn't left them on purpose. A weight lifted and was gone.

By now there was no path that Nettle could see, but the Woodfolk man loped on and on, sometimes resting one big hand against a tree as though it were a particular friend. "As old as rocks, these trees are," he said as they walked. "You've come to a good place."

At last he stopped. "There is it is," he said, pointing down a slope. "That little flat place."

There was no sign of trampled grass or chopped trees or

left-behind tent pegs lying around, but with Woodfolk there never was.

Bracken made a silver spell mark and left it shimmering on a tree where she could find it again, and where the Woodfolk would see it when they returned. Then there was nothing more to do but wait.

"How many moons until midwinter here?" asked Nettle.

"Three," said the Woodfolk man.

Bracken said it wasn't so long, really.

Every night Nettle and Bracken watched the moon out of their sleeping loft window. It was Nettle who noticed that the moon here was different.

Here, the new moon's crescent of pale silver faced the same way as the rim of her right thumbnail. And surely in the valley, the new moon had faced the other way? Nettle showed Bracken with her thumbnail. "The moon goes backwards here. It's a backwards moon."

"Hmm," said Bracken, looking up at it. "I think you're right."

"I wonder what Ben and the others are doing right now," Bracken said.

Nettle wondered about Elizabeth too, but there was no way of telling.

"Maybe when the Woodfolk come, they'll know where some other witches are," she said. "Ones our age, even."

Bracken nodded. "Maybe they will."

"You know, tomorrow we could go find some ravens. We could play the raven game. If they don't already know it, we could teach them."

"Maybe there are marmots here," said Bracken. "Or we could try talking to some sea lions, maybe."

"Otters," said Nettle. "*I* think otters would be way more interesting than sea lions."

They were still arguing when they went to bed, but it didn't matter, really. They had lots of days ahead of them.

And tomorrow would be a fine one for flying.